P9-DGK-800

ALBERT R. BROCCOLI's EON PRODUCTIONS Presents

PIERCE BROSNAN

as IAN FLEMING'S JAMES BOND *007* in

THE WORLD IS NOT ENOUGH

ALBERT R. BROCCOLI's EON PRODUCTIONS

Presents PIERCE BROSNAN

as IAN FLEMING'S JAMES BOND *007* in

"THE WORLD IS NOT ENOUGH"

SOPHIE MARCEAU   ROBERT CARLYLE

DENISE RICHARDS   ROBBIE COLTRANE and JUDI DENCH

Costume Designer	LINDY HEMMING
Music by	DAVID ARNOLD
Editor	JIM CLARK
Director of Photography	ADRIAN BIDDLE BSC
Production Designer	PETER LAMONT
Line Producer	ANTHONY WAYE
Written by	NEAL PURVIS & ROBERT WADE
Produced by	MICHAEL G. WILSON and BARBARA BROCCOLI
Directed by	MICHAEL APTED

DISTRIBUTED BY MGM DISTRIBUTION CO.

www.mgm.com

The World Is Not
Enough

A novel by
Raymond Benson

Based upon the screenplay by
Neil Purvis & Robert Wade

BERKLEY BOULEVARD BOOKS, NEW YORK

This is a work of fiction. Names, characters, places, and incidents are either the product of the author's imagination or are used fictitiously, and any resemblance to actual persons, living or dead, business establishments, events or locales is entirely coincidental.

THE WORLD IS NOT ENOUGH

A Berkley Boulevard Book / published by arrangement with
Ian Fleming (Glidrose) Publications Limited

PRINTING HISTORY
Berkley Boulevard edition / October 1999

The Penguin Putnam Inc. World Wide Web site address is
http://www.penguinputnam.com

ISBN: 0-425-17350-X

BERKLEY BOULEVARD
Berkley Boulevard Books are published by The Berkley Publishing Group, a division of Penguin Putnam Inc., 375 Hudson Street, New York, New York 10014.
BERKLEY BOULEVARD and its logo are trademarks belonging to Penguin Putnam Inc.

PRINTED IN THE UNITED STATES OF AMERICA

10 9 8 7 6 5 4 3 2 1

Acknowledgments

The author wishes to thank the following individuals for their help in preparing this book: Bruce Feirstein, Peter Lamont, James McMahon, and Moana Re Robertson.

Contents

I

Errand Boy

As he rode in the taxi from Bilbao's airport, James Bond's recollection of M's orders was clear enough. *Bring back Sir Robert's money.*

Nevertheless, Bond had a secondary objective in mind, and one that might prove to be slightly more of a risk. Initially, he had bristled at the notion of being a messenger boy for a wealthy oil tycoon, even if the man was a fellow Briton. He had to make sure that Sir Robert received a refund for a bad purchase he had made on the black market. Bond normally considered this kind of assignment a waste of time for someone in the Double-0 Section, but then he thought about how the job presented another, more appealing, opportunity.

Fine, he thought. He would get the money back—that

was not a problem. But it was more important to avenge the death of a fellow agent.

Double-O Twelve had been a recent recruit to SIS, and Bond had barely known him. Yet, when a fellow agent was murdered in the field, the entire Double-0 Section took it personally. It was like losing a member of the family. Even though M had warned Bond that entertaining notions of a vendetta might cloud his judgment on this particular assignment, 007 felt that it was his duty to even the score if he could.

It had begun yesterday with a summons from his chief. Bond had welcomed the interruption from the pile of intelligence reports he routinely absorbed in between assignments. Hoping that he was to be sent across the world on a potentially interesting case, or indeed, anything that would get him out of London, Bond had taken the lift to M's office in the SIS building on the Thames. Miss Moneypenny had offered no hint as to what the assignment was to be except that she was arranging for him to fly to Spain.

M was busy with a document on her desk when he walked in.

"Sit down, Double-0 Seven," she said, without looking up.

Over the past few years, Bond had strengthened his relationship with his relatively new boss at SIS. The new M had earned Bond's respect and loyalty. He liked to think he had earned hers.

However, when she said, "Sir Robert King needs an errand boy, and you're he," Bond blinked.

"Ma'am?" Bond wasn't sure that he had heard her correctly. "The oil tycoon?"

"That's right. He needs you to go to Bilbao tomorrow to pick up a caseful of money from a Swiss bank there. It's a refund for a secret report he bought on the black market. The document wasn't what he had been led to believe it was. He complained. The sellers agreed to a refund in good faith. An intermediary has requested that MI6 send someone to pick it up. I'd like you to do it, Double-0 Seven."

Bond frowned. He was not a person who kept up with the lives of Britain's rich and famous, but he knew enough about Sir Robert King to know that he was certainly high on the list of U.K. VIPs.

"Besides," M continued, "it would be a personal favor to me. Sir Robert is an old friend."

Bond was not surprised. M had friends in powerful places. She had come to SIS well connected and was able to play the politicians with more finesse than her predecessor ever cared to do. Even though she was the head of SIS, M was not averse to socializing with Britain's elite. In this day and age, it was probably wise intelligence policy.

Bond silently reviewed what he knew about the man. Sir Robert King, chief executive officer and chairman of King Industries Plc., had made a fortune over a quarter of a century ago from a lucrative construction business inherited from his father. When King married his second wife, whose family owned the remnants of a mismanaged oil importing firm, he slowly moved King Industries' interests toward petroleum production. Following the tragic death of his wife, King spent the next ten years saving the company's assets and tripling his income, as well as Britain's own oil supplies. He had become a national hero of sorts and had been knighted. Since that time, King Industries had become a major player in a worldwide, competitive business. King was always popping up in the British press. Bond's impression of him was that he was something of a charming rogue who enjoyed the life of a very rich, elderly playboy. Bond had never met the man, nor did he wish to.

And then there was the daughter . . .

"Whatever happened with the Elektra King kidnapping case?" Bond asked. "It isn't talked about much these days, is it?"

M looked at Bond with steel in her eyes. "That's completely irrelevant to your assignment, Double-0 Seven."

Bond blinked again. Had he touched some kind of nerve?

It had happened a little over a year ago. Elektra King, Sir Robert's glamorous daughter, a girl in her late twenties, had been kidnapped and held for ransom. At the time Bond had been out of the country on assignment. He didn't know much about the case, only that Miss King had been held for two or three weeks, and then had miraculously escaped on her own. Most of her captors were killed. He remembered that it had been reported in the British press and on the BBC, but the coverage disappeared from the news surprisingly fast considering the victim involved.

"I like to know all the facts before I walk into some-

4

thing, especially if it happens to be a Swiss bank," he said.

M was not amused. "MI5 took over the kidnapping case, as it occurred in this country. We have never had anything to do with it," M said. "As for the press, perhaps for once they respected the family's wishes not to be bothered about a painful and traumatic event. Thank God they left the poor girl alone after her ordeal. But never mind that. We *are* connected to this report Sir Robert bought. It was one of Double-0 Twelve's possessions. The report was stolen from his office when he was killed."

"Really?" Bond asked, interested now. News of 0012's murder in Omsk had sent a shock wave throughout the department. One of the few Double-0 agents who was permanently stationed abroad, 0012 was found shot dead in the Russian station a month earlier. The office had been ransacked and all classified material taken.

"I don't want you to go entertaining notions of a vendetta, Double-0 Seven," M warned. "It can cloud your judgment. Double-0 Twelve's murder is being investigated. Your assignment is to bring back Sir Robert's money."

With that she had dismissed him. Moneypenny provided him with his ticket, travel details, and the contact at the bank, a man named Lachaise. Before leaving the building, Bond visited Q Branch to pick up something he knew might be useful.

He had flown on Iberia Airlines into Bilbao the next morning, and now he was being whisked by taxi into the capital of Vizcaya province in northern Spain. The city's outskirts, near the airport, were a hub for maritime commerce and heavy industry. Bond was driven to the Casco Viejo, the nerve center bundled up on the right bank of the Ría de Bilbao, where he could see the municipality's characteristics change to a metropolitan cluster of banks and modern office buildings. During the day, the city retained a businesslike and somewhat elegant ambience not unlike that of some French provincial capitals. All that disappeared after sundown, for Bond could attest to the celebrated Spanish love for rowdy nightlong revelry in this particular city. He once had a memorable evening (and morning) with a fiery señorita in Bilbao. A flamenco dancer by profession, she had used what he could only best describe as "rhythmic charms" to demonstrate that Latin lovers really are warm-blooded.

The taxi pulled around Alameda de Mazarredo, where the Museo Guggenheim de Arte Contemporáneo is now the showpiece of the waterfront. One critic has described the spectacular titanium-skinned building, designed by American architect Frank Ghery, as a "cauliflower on LSD." Still, Bond couldn't help but be impressed with the shimmering, iconoclastic structure, which certainly seemed out of place in a city not known for its love of art. Too bad he hadn't the time to take a look at the collection, but he wasn't in Spain for that.

Bond dropped the taxi in the Plaza de Museo, then walked away from the Guggenheim toward a nearby rather nondescript office building. The engraved brass plaque in front announced LA BANQUE SUISSE DE L'INDUSTRIE (PRIVÉE). Underneath were translations in

Spanish, German, and English. Before entering, Bond slipped on the lightly tinted glasses that he had picked up from Q Branch, then made a quick check of his belongings, namely the Walther PPK under his navy sport jacket and a Sykes-Fairbairn throwing knife concealed in a sheath on his lower back.

He entered the building and gave his name to the mousy, horn-rimmed receptionist. She punched some buttons on her desk and spoke French into her headset. She nodded, then said to Bond, smoothly switching to English, "Mr. Lachaise will be with you momentarily." Bond smiled and sat down in the comfortable lounge. The Guggenheim could be seen in all its splendor across the plaza through a large wall-sized window.

Three Armani-clad thugs eventually appeared from behind a column. The suits were incongruous, for they looked more like professional wrestlers than bankers.

"Mr. Bond?" one of them grunted. "Come this way."

Bond stood and followed them into the lift. The three men stood silently around him, one man in front, blocking the doors.

"Nice day," Bond said. The men didn't acknowledge him.

The lift stopped at the top floor. The big men escorted Bond down a hallway, past an attentive secretary, and into a luxurious office, the focal point of which was a large oak desk. Behind the desk were three floor-to-ceiling windows that looked out onto a balcony and the street beyond.

Lachaise, an extremely well-groomed gentleman, was sitting at the desk studying figures on a printout.

"Mr. Bond," the head thug announced.

As if on cue, the other two men began to frisk Bond. They quickly found the Walther and set it on the desk. A few seconds later, they found the knife and laid it beside the other weapon.

The head man nodded to Lachaise that Bond was clean.

When this formality had been completed, Lachaise looked up with patronizing amusement and said, "Good. Now that we're all comfortable, why don't you sit down?" He gestured to a leather armchair, then sat back behind the desk. "So good of you to come to see me, Mr. Bond. Particularly at such short notice."

Bond said, "If you can't trust a Swiss banker, what's the world coming to?"

Lachaise laughed gently and punched a button. Bond dropped into the chair as a very attractive brunette entered the room, pushing a cart carrying a large silver metal case and a cigar box. She picked up the box and offered it to Bond. It was full of Havanas. He shook his head, keeping his attention on the banker. She then offered the box to Lachaise, who took a cigar and set it on the ashtray on the desk.

"Thank you, Giulietta," Lachaise said. He turned his attention to Bond. "It wasn't easy, but I retrieved the money. No doubt Sir Robert will be pleased to see it again."

The girl picked up the case and set it in Bond's lap. She opened it with a flourish, a seductive smile on her face during the entire process. The case was full of fifty-pound sterling notes.

"It's all there at the current exchange rate. Here is the statement."

Giulietta offered Bond a piece of paper, which he took and gave a cursory glance. It was an odd number, calculated down to the penny: £3,030,003.03.

"Would you like to check my figures?" the girl asked.

"I'm sure they're perfectly rounded," Bond replied. She was certainly not Swiss, Bond observed; she looked Mediterranean, with long, curly hair and large brown eyes. Spanish? Southern Italian, perhaps?

She closed the case and stepped back as Lachaise said, "It's all there, I assure you."

Bond slipped the statement into his pocket, then slowly and deliberately removed his glasses. He eyed Lachaise and, after a brief pause, said, "I didn't come only for the money. The report Sir Robert bought was stolen from an MI6 agent, who was killed for it."

Bond reached into another pocket and pulled out a photo of 0012. He laid it on the desk in front of Lachaise.

"I want to know who killed him."

Lachaise raised his eyebrows, attempting to register confusion and surprise, as if he had no idea what Bond was talking about. He glanced at the photo. After an obviously rehearsed moment of reflection, Lachaise went, "Tsk, tsk," nodded his head, and said, "Oh, right, quite so. Yes, terrible tragedy."

Bond looked at him hard, waiting for him to go on.

"But," Lachaise said, raising a finger, "not to put too fine a point on it, your MI6 agent had stolen the document himself, two weeks earlier, from a Russian operative."

As if that excused the killer.

"I want a name," Bond said.

Lachaise smiled, much too warmly. "Discretion, Mr. Bond. I'm a Swiss banker. Surely you can understand my position—"

"Which is what?" Bond snapped. "Neutral? Or just pretending to be?"

"I am merely a middleman. I'm just doing the honorable thing and returning the money to its rightful owner."

"And we know how difficult that can be for the Swiss," Bond said.

Lachaise dropped his smile. The two men stared at each other. The cigar girl and the three thugs felt the growing tension in the room.

Finally, the banker said, "I'm offering you the opportunity to walk out with the money, Mr. Bond."

"And I'm offering you the opportunity to walk out with your life," Bond replied.

"In your present situation," Lachaise said, indicating the three men behind Bond, "speaking strictly as a banker, of course, I'd have to say that the numbers are not on your side." He nodded to the first thug, who pulled a Browning Hi-Power 9mm handgun from beneath his jacket.

Carefully putting his glasses back on and fingering the frames, Bond said, "Perhaps you failed to take into account my hidden assets."

A flicker of doubt passed over Lachaise's face as

Bond's finger found a tiny protrusion on the arm of his glasses.

A charge inside the grip of the gun on the table flashed loudly and brightly, blinding everyone except Bond. It was a brief effect, just enough to disorient the thugs and give him the opening he needed. Bond jumped out of his seat, spear-handed the gunman in the throat and simultaneously grabbed the pistol with his other hand. The Browning discharged a shot, blowing out one of the windows behind the desk, but the gunman flew backward, unconscious. Without wasting a second, Bond turned and flung his leg up and out, kicking the second henchman in the face. The third man lunged at Bond, but he was too late. Bond spun around, took hold of the man's shoulders, and used the thug's own momentum to hurl him up and over the armchair and against a low cupboard. He then leaped over the desk and thrust the borrowed Browning into the hollow of Lachaise's cheek.

It all happened in six seconds. Lachaise hadn't had time to think.

"It seems you've had a small reversal of fortune," Bond said. "Give me a name."

Now truly frightened, Lachaise stammered, "I . . . I can't tell you . . ."

"Let's count to three," Bond said. "You can do that, can't you?" He cocked the gun, the click sending a shiver down the Swiss banker's spine. "One. Two—"

"All right!" Lachaise cried. "All right! But you must protect me!"

Bond said, "Fine. Now talk."

But the banker suddenly stiffened, his eyes wide. A

knife had been thrown, and it was now protruding grotesquely from the man's neck.

Giulietta the cigar girl had acted quickly and professionally. Now she leaped past the desk, through the broken window, and out onto the balcony. Bond pushed Lachaise to the floor and ran to the window. He saw that the brunette was swinging on a wire that she must have previously attached to the balcony railing. She sailed smoothly over the side street to another building. She quickly disappeared into the shadows before Bond could fire a shot. Already, there were sirens in the distance; the police had no doubt been alerted by the secretary outside the office. He had to move fast.

Bond turned, only to find that the first thug had recovered and was blocking the way, gun in hand. He was about to squeeze the trigger when Bond saw a red dot appear on the man's chest. Behind him, another window shattered as a bullet zinged through and pierced the henchman's heart. Bond instinctively ducked behind the desk and peered outside in an attempt to find the source of the shot, but there were too many windows in the building across the street.

He rolled over and up to run for the door, but he could hear voices and the sound of running feet in the hallway. Bond threw the bolt and quickly glanced at the windows again. Why wasn't the sniper shooting? He looked around the room and noted that the second thug was beginning to stir.

Bond realized that whoever had shot through the window had not been aiming at him. Perhaps the balcony was the safest escape route after all . . .

A breeze blew, fluttering the curtains that had been pulled back and tied with a long piece of decorative rope. Thinking quickly, Bond grabbed the rope, yanked it down, and threaded one end under a radiator pipe beneath a shattered window. He then moved to the prone body of the groggy henchman and tied the rope to his legs in a slipknot.

Shouting in Spanish followed a ferocious hammering at the door. The police had arrived.

Bond deftly picked up his Walther PPK and throwing knife and pocketed them, then clutched the handle on the caseful of money. He then wrapped the other end of the rope around his arm and eyed the window, ready to make his move.

He paused just long enough to take one of the Havanas from the box on the cart and slip it into his pocket.

Bond ran through the open window and leaped. He held on tightly to the case with one hand and gripped the rope with the other. In the office, the groggy henchman came to his senses in time to see the rope tied to his ankles running out of the window. He clung to the leg of the desk and held on for dear life as the rope went taut.

Bond's fall suddenly jerked to a stop.

Then the leg of the desk broke off in the thug's hand and Bond's weight dragged him across the Oriental rugs toward the window. He crashed into the wall just as the police burst through the door with their guns drawn.

Outside, Bond slowly descended to the street on the rope, unwrapped it, and dropped the remaining ten feet to the pavement. He rounded the corner to blend in with the lunchtime business crowds—just another man with a case, in a suit and tie.

As he walked, though, Bond glanced at the building where the cigar girl had fled. Why would someone up there want him to get out of that room alive?

While pondering this strange turn of events, he decided that perhaps he should take in some contemporary art after all. As more police poured into the bank building, Bond slipped into the front of the Guggenheim museum and disappeared.

He was back in London before midnight.

Giulietta entered the huge, high-ceilinged room in the building across from the Swiss bank. She swallowed hard, for she was terribly afraid of the man who was standing on the balcony overlooking the city.

He was not a large man. He was slight, thin and wiry, but there was no doubt that he could be quick on his feet. His cold eyes were as dark as anthracite. He might have been handsome at one time, but the raised, red scar on his right temple distorted the shape of his shiny, bald head. It was an ugly, slick wound that throbbed and shifted with the slightest facial expression, like an insect living just beneath the man's skin. His right eye drooped slightly, deadened. His mouth turned down on the same side, and he was unable to smile. As a result, he was quite literally a man with two half faces. It was a condition an unfortunate Syrian doctor had called Bell's palsy.

The girl approached him, but he didn't move. A gas-operated Belgian FN FAL sniper's rifle with an attached laser sight was propped against the doorframe. Binoculars on a tripod were trained on the rooftop below, where Bilbao policemen were now inspecting the shattered office windows.

"Renard . . ." Giulietta whispered.

The man seemed lost in thought. He rubbed and pinched his trigger finger, attempting to find a single nerve ending that might respond. He even brought the hand up to his mouth and bit the fleshy area between his thumb and forefinger. As always, he felt nothing.

Then he turned and inspected her. Finally, he said, "What's his name?"

The girl seemed to lose the ability to speak. Renard the Fox might very well kill her then and there.

"Our friend from MI6," he said quietly. "What's his name?"

Giulietta swallowed and finally found her voice. "James Bond."

Renard nodded as if he knew all about the Briton. "Ah. One of M's more resourceful tin soldiers."

"He . . . he could identify me," she said.

Renard reached out and touched her cheek. She tensed at the cold tips of his fingers.

The man looked at the girl in front of him. She was attractive, certainly, but he felt no desire for her. She was merely an expendable soldier.

"Then I suppose a death is in order," he said. He paused long enough for her eyes to widen, then dropped his hand. "His. When the time is right, I trust you won't fail."

She sighed with relief. He was giving her another

chance. Renard left the balcony and took a bottle of wine that was sitting on the bar of the suite. He filled two glasses and handed one to her.

"Until then, let us toast this James Bond." He raised the glass. "We're in his hands now."

Fireworks on the Thames

The Westland Lynx helicopter picked up Bond and made the short hop to central London, swooping over the spectacular Millennium Dome as it followed the river. Called the "dustbin lid" by some critics, the dome was the largest in the world, having been constructed on the North Greenwich peninsula, bounded on three sides by the River Thames. As Bond looked at the Teflon-coated glass-covered structure from the window, he was reminded of a giant robotic beetle with antennae that might have come from an episode of *Doctor Who*. Part of a three-hundred-acre former gasworks, the site had been derelict for more than two decades until it was sold to English Partnerships in 1997. Two Wembley Stadiums could fit inside the dome, which is tall enough to house Nelson's Column and big enough to accommodate forty thousand people. More significantly, the site was chosen because the Prime Meridian cuts across the west side, which is about two and a half kilometers from historic Greenwich.

As far as Bond was concerned, it added yet another eyesore to the otherwise lovely scenery around the Thames. Another, of course, was the gaudy, layer-cake-like building that was the headquarters of SIS in London.

The Lynx banked along the snaking river and landed near the river entrance of the SIS building. Carrying the money case, Bond disembarked, nodded at the police officer standing guard at the private entrance, then entered the secret, high-tech world that was MI6. Although all the security personnel knew Bond by sight, it was standard operating procedure that every precaution be taken. He passed through the metal detector, which clearly indicated that he was carrying his usual weaponry. An attentive staff member took the case from Bond and set it on a table. Bond opened it and began to scoop out the packs of cash. He wistfully flicked his finger through the last wad, then threw it down with the rest as a blue light scanned the money in three dimensions. Bond watched as the money was bundled into a clear plastic bag, sealed, and placed on a tray that was wheeled through a series of barred enclosures into a secure room. Bond handed the empty case to an attendant.

"Have this checked. See what you can get off it," he said.

"Yes, sir."

The money would be thoroughly checked for fingerprints and clues to its origins before it was handed over to Sir Robert. As there was a lot of it, the process could take some time.

Bond took the lift to his floor, nodded at his temporary personal assistant, and entered his private office. He quickly perused his mail and messages, then made his way back to the lift. Upstairs, he found Miss Moneypenny standing at one of the large filing cabinets in her outer office. Bond walked in with a smile, his arm hiding something behind his back.

She brightened at the sight of him. "James. Brought me a souvenir from your trip? Chocolates? An engagement ring?"

Bond revealed his hand, producing the cigar he had taken from the bank office in Bilbao. It was now inside a rather large, phallic tube. He stood it up on her desk.

"Thought you might enjoy one of these," he said.

"How romantic," she said, shoving the filing drawer closed. "I know exactly where to put it."

With a flourish, she tossed the cigar into the dustbin.

Bond sighed. "Ah, Moneypenny. That's the story of our relationship. Close, but no cigar."

She scowled at him as M's voice boomed through the intercom box on the desk.

"I hate to tear you away from affairs of state, Double-0 Seven. Would you mind coming in?"

Bond cleared his throat and replied, "Right away, ma'am."

As he walked toward the padded door, Moneypenny whispered, "Sure you don't want to give *her* the cigar, James?"

He shot her a look as he opened the door and entered the inner sanctum.

Bond was surprised to find that M was not alone. A distinguished-looking gentleman was with her, and Bond recognized him immediately.

M sat behind the desk, laughing at something the man had just said. Two glasses and an open bottle of malt whisky were between them. She regained her composure and gestured to them both. "James Bond, Sir Robert King."

King moved to shake hands with an easy, patrician smile. He was handsome, immaculately groomed, and appeared to be in his sixties.

"Ah!" he said. "The man who retrieved my money. Excellent job. Can't thank you enough."

The man's grip was warm and dry. Bond couldn't help but notice the shiny lapel pin King was wearing. It looked like the glass eye of a snake and was possibly very valuable.

King turned to M and teased, "Be careful, my dear. I might try to steal him from you."

Bond was put off by the man's presumptuousness.

"Construction's not exactly my specialty," he said with little humor.

"Quite the opposite, in fact," M couldn't resist quipping.

King smiled at Bond. "Oh, it's the oil business that makes our world go 'round now, Mr. Bond." He then turned and moved behind the desk in order to kiss M on the cheek.

"Give my best to your family," he said.

"We'll speak soon," M said.

He then bowed slightly to them both and left the room.

"Old friend, you say?" Bond asked.

"We read law at Oxford together," she explained as she stood and gathered the empty glasses and bottle of whisky. "Always knew he'd conquer the world." Before putting the glasses away, she had second thoughts. "Care for a drink?"

"Thank you."

She took a clean glass from a shelf behind the desk and poured whisky into it, handed it to Bond, then re-filled her own glass.

"He's a man of great integrity," M said, raising her glass to Bond.

"Who buys stolen reports for three million pounds."

She frowned. "Contrary to what you may believe, Double-0 Seven, the world is not populated by madmen who can hollow out volcanoes, fill them with big-breasted women, and threaten the world with nuclear annihilation."

Bond grinned at the irony of her remark as he stepped over to the ice bucket. He picked up two cubes and plopped them into his tumbler.

"It only takes one," he said.

M ignored the quip and walked around her desk, as-suming a relaxed position on the edge of it. "Any leads on the sniper?"

"No. The hotel room was clean. Professional job."

M pondered this as she took a sip from her drink.

Bond noticed a report on the desk that was stamped

with a strange seal. He took a closer look and saw that it was from the Russian Atomic Energy agency.

"Is that the stolen report?" he asked.

M nodded and handed it to him. Bond set down his tumbler and began to thumb through the document.

"Yes. Classified, from the Russian Atomic Energy Department. All it does is assess the computer bug threat on the nuclear arsenal in the former Soviet Republics."

Neither of them noticed that the ice in Bond's tumbler was beginning to fizz.

"What would King want this for?" he asked.

"As I told you before, it wasn't what he thought it was. He was led to believe the document was a secret report that identified the terrorists who've attacked a new oil pipeline he's building in the region. Kazakhstan . . . Azerbaijan . . . that part of the world. He's had quite a bit of trouble with bands of local tribesmen who get hold of explosives and vandalize his operations. He thought the report would pinpoint who the real culprits are and he could go to the proper authorities with it. But when he discovered the report concerned nuclear weapons, he turned it over to me, immediately. It turns out the thing's worthless. It's nothing new to us."

The ice continued to fizz, unnoticed.

"Interesting," Bond said. "So Sir Robert gave this worthless report to MI6, and *then* we received a call about the money?"

"That's right," M said, a bit perturbed that Bond was going back over details. "We received a message that Sir Robert could have his money back. All we had to do was send someone to Spain to pick it up from a Swiss banker. We sent you."

"It's all a bit of a mystery, isn't it? Everyone in that bank office died, except the girl. And me."

"Remember, you're the one who drew a weapon first. You might have come out of there with the money *and* without an incident. I already lost one Double-0 this month, I don't need to lose another."

Bond ignored the reprimand. "But why give back the money in the first place? It doesn't explain why someone wanted me to get out of that office in Bilbao alive . . . with the cash . . ." He paused for a moment, rubbing his thumb and forefinger together. It was then that he felt the strange bubbling where he had touched the ice. His eyes darted to the tumbler. The ice was boiling!

What the hell? he thought. He sniffed his fingers, identified the smell, then dropped the report on the desk. "King! The money! M, it's a bomb!"

Bond was halfway out of the door when M stabbed at the intercom. "Moneypenny! Stop King!"

Sir Robert and an MI6 aide were unaware of the sudden alarm as they walked toward the security area of the building. King's only thoughts were on the money, which was still lying on the tray, wrapped in plastic. Security bars were between him and the cash. An official produced a bag and moved toward it, saying, "We haven't finished checking it yet, sir."

Sir Robert waved him away. "I'm sure it's all there. If you can't trust MI6, whom can you trust?"

The official hesitated a moment, then decided not to argue with one of the more powerful men in Britain. He placed the money inside a canvas bag, opened the gate, and handed the cash to King.

"Thank you," the tycoon said. He heaved the bag over his shoulder. "Quite heavy, isn't it?" he said to the aide, and proceeded to walk alone into the corridor leading outside.

Bond, rushing through the building, took a shortcut through the Q Branch laboratory, where Major Boothroyd and his technicians were busy working on a strange, half-built boat suspended over a water tank. Q was startled as Bond ran past them.

"Where's the fire, Double-0—?" Boothroyd asked, but Bond was already gone.

He rounded a corner, took a flight of stairs three steps at a time, and bolted into the security area. "Stop! King!" he shouted.

But the call was muffled where King was walking. His mind was so focused on the money that even he didn't hear the serene hum that his lapel pin began to emit.

Bond reached the lower corridor's open doorway just as a massive explosion rocked the building, and all hell broke loose. Fire blasted out of the corridor, knocking Bond back and to the floor. The entire structure shook for a moment as a lower tier gave way, its roof and a wall collapsing amid the smoke and flames.

Giulietta the cigar girl sat in a Sunseeker Hawk 34 at the edge of the Thames, eyeing the destruction that was caused by the little device that Renard had created. The fools at MI6 had fallen for it, hook, line, and sinker. She picked up the FN FAL sniper rifle and lined up the infrared telescopic sight with the billow of dark smoke that was pouring out of the hole in the building.

Just as Renard had predicted, James Bond stumbled out of the wreckage, peering around and attempting to find the source of the mayhem. She took careful aim and activated the laser.

Bond coughed and rubbed smoke from his eyes, shaken from the blast but unharmed. But Sir Robert and a small section of SIS headquarters had vanished in the blink of an eye. The culprits had to be nearby, watching.

He waved the smoke away and then noticed the wand of red light pointing at his chest. Instinctively he dived for cover just as the powerful, high-velocity bullets blanketed the area. He crawled behind a stone wall, drew the Walther, and prepared to return fire. He scanned the area but the bullets continued to fly over his head. Bond snaked on his belly a little farther out so that he could see more clearly.

She was on a sleek high-tech boat, approximately a hundred yards from the shore. He immediately recognized her as the girl from Bilbao.

Realizing that she had failed to kill the MI6 agent, Giulietta's only goal now was to get out of there alive. She dropped the rifle and gunned the engines, speeding off down the river.

Determined, Bond jumped up and raced back into the wreckage and chaos that the building had become. Q was not going to like it, but there was only one thing to do.

The Q Branch boat had been lowered into the tank, temporarily forgotten, and now Major Boothroyd and his men were busy checking reports of damage, sounding alarms and sealing off passages. They didn't notice James Bond as he ran into the room and leaped into the boat.

Bond stared at the mystifying number of buttons and gadgets on the console, gambled and pressed a red button. The engine roared and the boat shot out of its berth.

Boothroyd looked up in horror. "Wait! It's not finished!"

The vessel, a one-man sprint boat that was compact, slim-lined, and built from scratch, soared out of the SIS rubble and into the Thames. The craft was lightweight and very sensitive to Bond's guidance. It spun around in the water, out of control, but Bond gripped the steering wheel and pulled it hard to the right. The boat leveled out, but its momentum nearly caused it to capsize. It took Bond approximately twenty seconds to get the feel of the controls, and then he steered the boat in the direction of the escaping assassin. He revved the engine and tore through the water after her.

Giulietta could see Bond's boat in a side mirror. He was gaining fast. She pushed her own engines to the limit, roaring to a new level of speed. The Hawk 34 was a luxury vessel capable of fifty-four knots, but Giulietta found that the boat's many extras—a full camper/suntop and tonneau, wet bar, refrigerator—were a liability now. It was meant to be a pleasure cruiser, not an escape boat. Still, the craft propelled through the water with immense power and strength. Giulietta thought that perhaps she could use the sheer size of the boat to her advantage.

Bond shot past two police boats that immediately

sounded alarms and gave chase behind the bizarre arrowhead-shaped green vessel. Police-car sirens were already wailing along the embankment; some emergency vehicles headed toward the SIS building, others followed the boat chase from the shore.

There were a surprising number of boats on the Thames. The cigar girl weaved in and out, almost ramming a small speedboat in the process. Bond was losing ground, but in a bid to keep pace, he corralled the boat into a hair-raising shortcut, shooting underneath a pier. He was barely able to maneuver the boat under it, but he luckily emerged even closer to his prey.

Enough is enough, the girl thought. She killed the motor, moved to the back of the boat, and pulled a tarpaulin off a rear-mounted machine gun. She snapped on the belt, took aim at Bond, and fired.

The Q Boat continued at full speed, now up to nearly seventy knots. The bullets bounced off the chobam armor plating that Bond knew covered the surface. He set his jaw and kept going, headed straight for her.

The girl remained calm and cool, shooting with precision. Why weren't the bullets penetrating? He was getting closer . . . closer . . .

Her eyes widened when she realized his boat was not going to stop. She let out a small scream and hit the deck as Bond steered his boat right over the machine gun and turret, using the girl's boat as a ramp. The Q Boat launched into the air, then dived, nose first, into the Thames.

She raised herself in time to see Bond turning the little powerhouse to close in for the kill. She scrambled to the helm, fired the engine again, and sped toward Tower Bridge, which was just beginning to open to allow for the passage of a small freighter.

Bond lagged behind, impeded by the influx of heavy traffic on the water. He watched helplessly as her boat was lost in the distance. Desperate, he looked around him and saw that a shore-side fish market was not far to his left. Gritting his teeth, he cranked the wheel and veered off, up a slipway and onto the embankment. The ingenuity of the Q Boat design allowed it to hydroplane on the pavement, propelling him through the market and into a busy London street. Pedestrians screamed and jumped out of the way as he wrestled with the controls, jetting off the street and straight toward a riverside restaurant full of people.

The boat crashed through the side of the restaurant, sending diners leaping in every direction. Waiters shouted at him, but before they knew what had happened, Bond's boat had sprung out over a balcony and splashed down once more into the Thames.

She was back in his sights.

Giulietta turned back, amazed that Bond had managed to overtake her. She bore down and kept going.

The racing boats sliced through an armada of lazy, overloaded barges, barely missing one and sending a small tidal wave over another. Then . . . they were at an even pace. Giulietta attempted to force her way past him, but Bond punched some buttons on the console of the Q Boat and released a set of catapulting flame canisters. They shot out ahead, creating a massive wall of fire in front of them.

Giulietta swerved her boat away from the flames just in time and was forced to turn toward the very edge of the river. She knew the chase was nearly over and that she had lost, but then she saw the huge, colorful hot-air balloon looming in the sky in front of her.

Their boats were now only yards away from the Millennium Dome. A crowd of people was gathered around the balloon, which was apparently about to launch. She skidded her vessel to a stop at the nearby pier and quickly scrambled out.

A flamboyant, wealthy celebrity was preparing to climb into the basket of the balloon. He waved to the crowd and smiled for the cameras, but Giulietta pushed through and leaped into the basket.

"Hey!" the man shouted, but she shoved him away. In one swift move, she cranked open the gas nozzles and the balloon rose with surprising speed.

Bond steered his craft toward a slipway adjacent to the pier, punched a button, and shot into the air. The crowd below watched with open mouths and unbelieving amazement.

The Q Boat sailed through the air just beneath the rising balloon. With split-second precision, Bond reached up and grabbed one of the ropes dangling from the balloon. The boat fell away, hitting the ground and erupting into a ball of flame. The crowd screamed and began to disperse. Few, though, could take their eyes off the man who was now being carried precariously through the air.

The balloon soared higher and higher. Giulietta pulled a Beretta from a holster at her side and fired over the

side of the basket. Bond swung back and forth underneath, like a pendulum, avoiding the bullets and praying
that she didn't get lucky. He strained to pull himself
upward as the arc of his swing under the basket provided
cover.

Giulietta continued to fire but stopped when she heard
the rumbling noise approaching the balloon. Looking up,
she was terrified to see three Westland Lynx police helicopters closing in on her.

Bond was getting closer to the bottom of the basket.

Giulietta pulled a knife from a sheath on her ankle
and considered going for Bond's rope. Instead, since the
helicopters were looming, she decided there was only
one alternative.

Bond's arm appeared over the rim of the basket. He
looked up just in time to see the girl slash one of the
gas hoses. A loud hiss drowned out all other noise as
the balloon filled not with hot air, but with gas. As she
put her hand on the flame regulator valve, Bond realized
what she was planning to do.

"Stop!" he shouted. "Don't! I can protect you!"

The brunette beauty simply looked at Bond and gave
him a sad smile.

"Not from *him*," she said.

She pulled on the regulator. Bond pushed himself
away from the basket as a four-foot lick of flame shot
up into the balloon. He plummeted downward as the
balloon exploded in a massive fireball, taking Giulietta
the cigar girl with it. The police helicopters swerved out
of the way just in time, avoiding further disaster.

Bond fell with a spectacular, thudding bounce onto

the roof of the Millennium Dome, landing hard on his left shoulder. He slid uncontrollably down the slope of the dome as scraps of the burning balloon rained down all around. A gutter eventually broke his fall.

Sitting up, he winced in searing pain and held on to his injured shoulder. He gazed at the massive smoke cloud in the sky, cursing the foolish girl and his own failure to stop her from destroying herself.

Bond also swore silently at the mystery man behind the blatant attempt to attack MI6 on its home turf. This time, he had gone too far.

3
Elektra

The memorial service was held at Sir Robert King's massive country estate near the shores of Loch Lomond, the largest freshwater lake in Britain. Located eighteen miles north of Glasgow and the River Clyde and straddling the geological fault that separates the Highlands from the Lowlands, the lake's beauty has attracted celebrated writers down the centuries.

On this sad occasion mourners from all over the world were drawn to Loch Lomond. They were the mighty and the powerful, the rich and famous . . . all dressed in black.

A nineteenth-century chapel in the grounds of the estate was the site of the service. The funeral was a grand, solemn affair, complete with bagpipe lament, sincere tributes by friends and associates, and even a message from the Queen.

James Bond, his left arm in a sling, was slightly late arriving. He had driven his Aston Martin DB5 to Scotland at breakneck speed, was waved through the heavily guarded checkpoint at the front of the estate, and arrived just as the mourners were filing out of the chapel. He slipped into the throng and moved a few steps behind Miss Moneypenny, who was with Bill Tanner and Charles Robinson, M's Chief of Staff and top analyst, respectively.

When the breathtakingly beautiful young woman appeared in the doorway of the chapel, all eyes were drawn to her. She was tall and shapely, had shoulder-length brown hair, piercing brown eyes, and a pouty, soft mouth. Bond was immediately mesmerized by her; although he had seen photographs, he had never viewed the girl in person. She walked through the crowd, head high, like a young Jacqueline Kennedy, dispensing solace and consolation to those around her. She was clearly the center of attention.

Robinson, a young black man who had joined MI6 only two years before, whispered to Moneypenny, "I couldn't help but notice that young woman during the service."

Bond moved next to him and said, "King's daughter. Elektra."

Robinson's expression said it all. She was indeed beautiful.

Elektra King was in her late twenties, but she had the manner of a woman ten years older. Behind the brown eyes was a sense that she had been to hell and back and lived to tell about it. There was a profound sadness there, and Bond knew that this was not just because she had lost her father.

He couldn't keep his eyes off her as she went from person to person, kissing a cheek, accepting a hug . . . and when she embraced M, Bond felt a sense of responsibility and pain.

M put her arm around Elektra and began walking with her, just the two of them. As M had been close to Sir Robert, it seemed only natural that she was protective and something of a maternal figure to the girl, who had lost her mother years ago to cancer.

Bond watched them move toward the shore of the lake. Inexplicably, the feeling of guilt gave way to one of apprehension, and he didn't know why.

That afternoon, the entourage from MI6 drove to Castle Thane, SIS's remote operations center in Scotland. Originally built in 1220 by Alexander II as a defense against the Vikings, the castle subsequently became a stronghold of the Mackenzies of Kintail (later the Earls of Seaforth), who installed the MacRaes as hereditary keepers. It had been destroyed in 1719 while being used as a garrison for Spanish troops fighting for the Jacobite cause on behalf of the fifth Earl of Seaforth, and restoration work wasn't performed until over two hundred years later. Shortly after the old M's retirement, SIS purchased a wing that was now off-limits to tourists, complete with a private, heavily guarded entrance. The current M felt a certain kinship with Scotland and had spearheaded the deal with the government. As she had settled in to her job as head of MI6 over the last few years, M exerted more and more authority over the way things were done at headquarters. One of the recent changes she had made was establishing the ability to be mobile. She had grown weary of London and had on many occasions looked for excuses to be elsewhere. Now, with the remote operations center in Scotland, she was free to come and go as she pleased, dragging her staff with her.

M had called the briefing for the afternoon of the funeral, knowing full well that if SIS were going to act on Sir Robert's assassination, they had to do it quickly. Every available Double-0 agent was present, including Bond, as well as Tanner, Robinson, Moneypenny, and other important members of staff. They sat in a vast stone room that was dominated by a huge, sparkling chandelier, as well as electronic equipment that looked decidedly out of place in the historic building. Every agent in the room, save for Bond, had a briefing packet on the desk in front of them.

Tanner's voice echoed in the chamber. "Our analysts have worked round the clock to determine exactly what happened in London. There was very little for MI5 to work with after the explosion. Their forensics team found traces of the bag of money, and performed tests to determine that the cash had been dipped in urea, dried, and packed tight. In effect, a highly compacted fertilizer bomb." Tanner registered a nod at Bond. "Having handled the money, the water on Double-0 Seven's hands—when he touched the ice in M's office—started a chemical reaction. That's what tipped him off to the bomb's composition."

Bond reflected on the bizarre moment when he had felt the sizzling sensation and saw the whisky boiling in the tumbler. If only he had noticed it a minute or two earlier . . .

Tanner continued, "How the explosive was set off was a matter of speculation until we found a transmitter in the woman's boat. What we think happened was that the metal anticounterfeiting strip on one of the notes had been replaced with magnesium, which acted as the detonator."

He picked up King's lapel pin, which was now blackened, fused, and melted to expose electronics beneath. "King wore a lapel pin like this. He called it the 'Eye of the Glens,' and it's apparently some kind of heirloom. He had had it forever. A good-luck charm of some sort. Obviously, it's not the original. King's real Eye of the Glens had been switched for this copy. We were very lucky that MI5 were able to find this piece of evidence amidst the . . . mess. It contained a radio receiver/transmitter that triggered the blast. In other words, the girl set off the bomb that killed him with the counterpart to the transmitter that we found in the boat she left behind on the Thames. All she had to do was turn it on and point the antenna at the SIS building. The signal activated the receiver in King's lapel pin. The pin then transmitted an electronic signal to the magnesium strip in the money."

A photograph of Giulietta the cigar girl appeared on the screen.

"She was identified as Giulietta da Vinci, an Italian national who was on Interpol's list of known terrorists operating in the Mediterranean. We have no further information on the woman. We don't know who she was working for."

Robinson stood beside Tanner and said, "We know it was someone close to King who switched his pin. Our only lead committed suicide in that balloon. Given the size of King's organization, it could be anyone. Anywhere." He turned to M and nodded, indicating that he and Tanner were finished.

M stood and took a moment to look at her people. Everyone in the room felt the coming harsh words even before she spoke.

"This will not stand," she said firmly. She allowed this to sink in, then continued. "We will not be terrorized . . . by cowards who would murder an innocent man . . . and use *us* as a tool."

Her eyes scanned the room. "You each have an assignment. We will find the people who committed this atrocity. We will hunt them, we will track them, we will follow them—to the far corners of the earth if need be—and we *will* bring them to justice."

She waited a beat, held her head high, then turned on her heels and left the room.

The other agents opened their briefing packets. Bond looked around him, realizing that he was the odd man out. As Tanner walked past, Bond stopped him.

"Bill . . . ?"

Tanner motioned to the sling. "Sorry, James. M says

you're off the active-duty list until you're cleared by medical."

Bond made an expression that questioned the wisdom of the decision. Tanner held up his hands as if to say that there was nothing he could do about it, then followed M out of the room.

Bond sat there a moment, watching his peers reading the material intently. *Well!* he thought. He would just have to get medical to clear him. And he knew just how to do it.

Bond refused to tease Dr. Molly Warmflash about her name, but the attractive young SIS medical officer certainly lived up to it. Ever since the firm hired her three months earlier, she had become the butt of countless jokes among the male population at headquarters. The problem was that she encouraged them. She was a flirt and enjoyed it. She had specifically chatted up Bond on several occasions, making it clear that she would like to examine him in much more detail than was appropriate in a professional environment. Bond wondered how long a girl like her would last in the organization, but so far she had also proven herself to be quite capable when it came to medical matters.

Dr. Warmflash was blond, petite, and curvy. Her stethoscope didn't merely hang around her neck—it jutted straight out and then dangled like a medal she might have won at an athletic event. Her blue eyes were full of life, confident, and bewitching.

Bond concentrated on all of these attributes as he sat on the examination table with his shirt off, while she poked and prodded his left shoulder. He tried his best not to flinch, but it hurt like hell.

"Dislocated collarbones take time, James," she said. "It's no better than the last time I looked at it. If any more tendons slip . . ."

She knew he was resisting showing the pain. To prove a point, she thrust a finger into a particularly sensitive area.

"Ow," Bond said, giving in to the discomfort.

Dr. Warmflash shook her head. "I'm afraid you're going to be out of action for weeks."

"Molly," he said, "I need a clean bill of health. You have to clear me for duty."

This time, she placed her fingers gently on the scarred and bruised bone. "James, it wouldn't really be . . ."

Bond laid a hand on her waist. "Ethical?"

She gave him a look.

"Can't we just skirt the issue?" he asked with a smile.

She glanced down at his hand, then returned the smile. Her eyes gave away the temptation. "You'd have to promise to call me," she said after thinking about it— for a couple of seconds. She jabbed him in the shoulder again, causing him to wince. "This time."

Bond said, "Whatever the doctor orders . . ."

She moved closer to him. He could smell her perfume. "And I suppose if you stayed in constant contact . . ."

Taking that as an invitation, Bond pulled at the zipper on her skirt. He expertly flicked the clasp and the garment fell to the floor. She was wearing white silk panties, a garter belt, and white stockings. The creamy flesh of her exposed thighs was begging to be caressed. He reached up and began to unbutton her blouse from the bottom. She helped him, working down from the top.

"If you showed sufficient . . . stamina . . ." she said, breathlessly.

The blouse was off, revealing magnificent breasts in a white, lace Wonderbra that seemed to be a size too small. Now the passion was insurmountable.

"And cut out all kinds of—" she said, but by then he had pulled her toward him. Their mouths met for twenty seconds.

When their lips parted, he whispered, "Strenuous activity?"

She pushed him back on the examination table and climbed on top. She kissed him again . . . and again . . . and again . . .

"I might be"—she gasped as his right hand stroked her backbone, finding the clasp to the bra and unsnapping it—"open to that—"

They kissed again.

"Good," Bond said, feeling her hand at his trousers. "I'd want you to stay on top of things."

An hour later, Bond left the doctor's office, pausing long enough to remove the sling and casually drape it on a suit of armor that stood silently guarding a corridor.

"The things we do for England," he said to it. "Carry on."

The distant sound of bagpipes caught Bond's attention. He had a good idea where it was coming from.

He quietly moved along the ancient corridors and down a flight of stone stairs. He came upon a man in full Scottish regalia, blaring away, rather badly.

"Get on with it," a familiar voice commanded.

The man in the kilt dropped the pipe from his mouth and simultaneously fired bullets from one pipe and a jet of flame from another. The target was a realistic dummy twenty feet away, which quickly became a molten, bullet-ridden mess.

"I suppose we all have to pay the piper sometime, right, Q?" Bond quipped.

"Pipe down, Double-0 Seven," Major Boothroyd said, more annoyed than usual.

"Was it something I said?"

"No." Boothroyd folded his arms. "Something you destroyed."

It was then that Bond noticed the mangled Q Boat sitting in the middle of the laboratory.

"My fishing boat," Boothroyd said. "For my retirement. Away from *you*."

"Had I known, I would have returned it in . . . what do you say . . . 'pristine condition'?"

Boothroyd shuddered. "Grow up, Double-0 Seven."

Q Branch never slept. There were always technicians working round the clock. Major Boothroyd, who was looking forward to the day he would finally retire, loathed leaving London for the remote Castle Thane. Nevertheless, when M called, naturally he came. He was tired and irritated.

"Come over here. Let's get this over with. It's past my bedtime," he said. "I want you to meet the young man I'm grooming to follow me."

He led Bond to a pool table, which, with the press of

a button, parted. The floor opened to reveal a rising platform, and on it was a brand-new battleship-gray BMW Z8 with a black convertible top. A man was loading a missile into one of the side grilles, but he didn't notice that the tail of his white lab coat was caught in the door. When he realized it, he turned the wrong way to get out.

Bond and Boothroyd exchanged a look.

"It helps if you open the door," Bond suggested, reaching for the handle and releasing the man.

The man turned to Bond and asked imperiously, "And you might be . . . ?"

"This is Double-0 Seven," Boothroyd said.

"If you're Q," Bond said to Boothroyd facetiously, "does that make him R?" He knew full well, of course, that "Q" stood for "Quartermaster."

The deputy controlled himself and said, "Ah, yes. The legendary Double-0 Seven wit. I, of course, am laughing *inside*. But I daresay you've met your match in this machine."

The man was very tall, had a high forehead and a mustache. Bond noticed the sunglasses in his pocket and took the liberty of examining them.

"New model? Improved specs?" he asked.

"I thought you were on the inactive roster. Some kind of injury," the deputy said.

Bond picked up the glasses and shrugged. "We'll see about that." He motioned to the car. "Do go on."

"As I was saying . . ." the deputy said as he stepped around the car. "The absolute latest in intercepts and countermeasures. Titanium armor, a multitasking heads-up display, six beverage-cup holders . . . All in all, rather stocked."

" 'Fully loaded' I think is the term," Q said. "Why don't you try on that coat for Double-0 Seven?"

The deputy hesitated, then walked over to a table and began to put on a sleek, black jacket.

Boothroyd gestured to the sunglasses and said, "You're right. New refinement. Sort of X-ray vision. For checking concealed weapons." He then led Bond to another table and handed him an Omega watch. "Your nineteenth, I believe? Try not to lose this one, all right? It has dual lasers and a miniature grappling hook with fifty feet of high-tensile filament, able to support eight hundred pounds."

Bond was impressed, slipping it on his wrist. They turned back to the deputy when he said, "That's odd."

He was looking down at something on the jacket. "Somebody forgot to remove this tag . . ." He yanked on it, and the jacket *snapped* abruptly to become an airbag. It enveloped him, impossibly ensnaring the man.

"He seems well suited for the job," Bond said to Boothroyd. They moved out of the laboratory and found a quiet place in the lab. Bond asked, "You're not retiring anytime soon, are you, Major?"

"Pay attention, Double-0 Seven," Boothroyd said, looking at Bond with a hint of mischief in his eyes. "There are two things I've always tried to teach you. First: never let them see you bleed."

"And second?" Bond asked.

"Always have an escape plan," the major said. A sudden whoosh of smoke enveloped Boothroyd as an ancient trapdoor in the wall opened behind him. When the smoke cleared, Q was gone.

The Research Department was a remote version of the recently installed Visual Library at the London headquarters, a computerized encyclopedia on a grand scale. One merely had to punch in a topic and the Visual Library would find every file available on the subject and organize it into a cohesive multimedia presentation.

Bond wanted to look into the story of Elektra King's kidnapping. As M had said, the story had disappeared from the news remarkably quickly. All he knew was that she had escaped and the kidnappers had been killed— except for the leader, who somehow got away.

He began by going over the history of Robert King's rise to fame and fortune. The monitor displayed photographs, newspaper clippings, magazine articles, and television snippets—all to do with King's life and times. King Industries seemed to be always in the news, especially in the financial sections of the papers. The knighthood was covered extensively. The press had made a big deal out of his second marriage. The birth of their daughter, Elektra, had also been big news.

Bond turned his attention to information relating to Elektra. While her early life was not too detailed, there were the occasional reports of her growth into adulthood—a photo from her sixteenth birthday, a brief article on her going up to university, and a small piece in *The Times* when she joined King Industries in hopes of following in her father's footsteps in the family business. She had grown up all over the world, apparently—a boarding school in Paris, university in Scotland, summers and holidays in the Middle East with her mother's family, and later, at her father's villa in Azerbaijan.

The next story, though, was the dominant one. It started with a newspaper headline that screamed, ELEKTRA KING KIDNAPPED!

Bond clicked on the "Police Files" icon and found a Polaroid that had been sent to Robert King by the captors. It showed Elektra, savagely beaten, bruised, her ear bandaged. She was holding the newspaper with the KIDNAPPED! headline. Beneath the photo, someone had scrawled the ransom figure—"$5,000,000."

According to Elektra's statement to the police, she had decided early on that she would risk her life to escape. At one point during the ordeal, she had kicked one of the kidnappers in the groin. While he was doubled up on the floor, she took his gun and shot him with it. She killed another captor and literally blasted her way out of the country cottage in Dorset where they had kept her hidden. Unfortunately, the leader of the team was not present at the time and had gotten away. Elektra had stumbled blindly to the main road, where a lorry driver had picked her up and taken her to a police station.

Bond clicked on the "Police Interview" icon. Elektra appeared on the monitor, shaken, emotional, near hysterics. Her wounds had been treated, but she looked terrible. Tears ran down her face.

"Tell me again how you got the gun," the interrogator probed gently.

"How many bloody times do I have to tell you?" Elektra cried. "There was one guy who was trying to molest me . . . he came into my room . . . my *cell* . . . and tried to touch me."

"And this was at night?"

"Early morning. The sun was just coming up, I think. It was up when I got out of the house."

"And what happened?"

"Like I said before . . ." She took a deep breath and began the story again. "I let him go just so far . . . so he would be overconfident. Then I kicked him hard in the crotch. When he doubled over on the floor, I pulled the gun away from him and shot him."

"And then . . ."

"I heard shouts and running. The others were coming to see what had happened. I aimed the gun at the door. As soon as it opened, I pulled the trigger."

"And how many men were there?"

"Two. I shot them both."

"What about the leader?" the interrogator asked. "The one who escaped. Can you describe him?"

"Bald. Dark eyes. He shouted," Elektra sobbed. "He shouted all the time . . ."

Touched, Bond froze the screen and lightly ran his fingers over Elektra's still face, attempting to will the tears away. Such a beautiful girl . . . it was a horrible . . .

Then a thought occurred to Bond. He flipped back to the Polaroid with the ransom figure. Five million dollars.

He reached into his pocket and removed his wallet. He took out the statement that the cigar girl had given to him in Bilbao. In all of the confusion after the explosion, Bond had completely forgotten about it. There it was, that strange number—£3,030,003.03. Something bristled at the back of his neck.

Bond tapped some keys, and the words EXCHANGE RATE—POUNDS TO DOLLARS appeared on the screen. He entered 3,030,003.03 POUNDS STERLING and hit return.

The result was 5,000,000 U.S. DOLLARS. He stared at it a moment, contemplating what this might mean. He typed some more, and an MI6 screen appeared that read ELEKTRA KING FILE 7634733. He pressed return and the monitor filled with the words ACCESS DENIED.

Bond frowned. He repeated the entire action and got the same result.

He sat back in the chair, perplexed. He fingered the statement in his hands and came to the only conclusion that was possible.

Bond paced the floor outside the Briefing Room, debating with himself if he should do what he felt he must. She must know the complete story. Would she agree to share it with him?

Throwing caution to the wind, he rushed past Moneypenny without saying a word, opened the door, and found M huddled with Tanner, Robinson, and two other government officials.

She looked up. "Yes, Double-0 Seven?"

"Tell me more about the kidnapping of Elektra King," he said.

M straightened, trying not to appear defensive. "I wasn't aware you had an assignment on this case—"

"I brought the money in that killed King."

"Don't make this personal."

"I'm not. Are you?" He paused a moment, then added, "You're the only one who could seal her file. MI5 is handling the case? I think not."

She hesitated a moment, then turned to Tanner and the others. "Would you excuse us?"

After they had left, she stared Bond down. "I will not tolerate insubordination, Double-0 Seven."

He shrugged, acknowledging that he had stepped over the line. He took a softer line, asking, "What happened?"

M looked away, obviously troubled. Then she came out with it. "When Elektra King was kidnapped, her father tried to deal with it on his own. With no success."

Bond waited.

"So he came to me," she said. "As you are aware, we do not negotiate with terrorists. And against every instinct in my heart—every emotion I have as a mother—I told him not to pay the ransom. I thought we had time on our side."

"You used the girl as bait."

"Yes."

"You thought you could smoke out the kidnappers."

"Once we learned who was behind it, yes."

Bond let the penny drop, and then said, "The amount of money in King's case was the same as the ransom demand for his daughter." He handed her the statement and watched as she studied it. "It was a setup. Giving the money back. The sniper in Spain made sure I got out of that office alive because he wanted *MI6* to deliver a bomb to King. It's a message to MI6, M. Your terrorist is back."

She looked up at him, concern deep in her eyes.

"Then we know who killed Double-0 Twelve . . . and King."

It was nearly midnight by the time they had reassembled in the Briefing Room. Tanner and Robinson had rushed to put together the necessary audio-visual aids so that M could shift directions on the case.

The wall screen filled with the face of a slight, thin, and wiry man. He was bald and had dark, cold eyes.

"Victor Zokas," M said. "Aka . . ."

"Renard the Fox," Bond said. "The anarchist."

Tanner picked up the briefing. "He was operating in Moscow in 1996, Pyongyang, North Korea, before that, and he's been spotted in Afghanistan, Bosnia, Iraq, Iran, Beirut, and Cambodia."

"All the romantic vacation spots," Bond noted.

"His only goal is chaos," the Chief of Staff continued. "Works as a freelancer. Has ties with the Russian Mafia."

"He was the mastermind behind Elektra King's kidnapping. After Sir Robert came to me," M said, "I sent Double-0 Nine to kill Renard. Before he completed the mission, Elektra had escaped. A week later, our man caught up with the target in Syria. Put a bullet in his head." She paused for effect. "Apparently, the bullet is still there."

"How did he survive?" Bond asked.

Tanner punched a button on the control panel and a huge, transparent, holographic 3-D image of Renard's skull appeared, floating in the center of the room.

"We *thought* he was dead," Tanner said. "We had

50

closed the file on Renard and had mistakenly ignored two reports claiming that he had been seen in Afghanistan and Azerbaijan. Just an hour ago, we received confirmation from our station in Turkey that Renard is indeed alive."

M nodded to Dr. Molly Warmflash, who was standing nearby. She stepped out of the shadows to explain. "The Syrian doctor who saved Renard couldn't get the bullet out, so Renard killed him."

Dr. Warmflash took over the controls and rotated the hologram. The bullet could be seen in the X ray, just inside the right temple.

"We got hold of the doctor's X rays of Renard's skull. The bullet is moving through the medulla oblongata, killing off his senses. Touch, smell—I would imagine that he feels no pain. I would bet that many of his facial muscles are paralyzed with Bell's palsy. But he can also probably push himself harder, longer than any normal man. The bullet will eventually kill him—but he'll get stronger every day, until the moment he dies."

M took over. "Robert is dead. MI6 is humiliated. Surely he has his revenge."

"Not quite," Bond said. "Renard had three enemies in that kidnapping. Sir Robert King, MI6 . . . and the one he hasn't touched. Elektra."

M flinched at Bond's frightening, but obviously correct, assumption. "There's another aspect to all this that I'm just beginning to realize," she said.

"What is that?"

"As heir to her father's vast global oil empire—Elektra King is arguably the most powerful woman in the world."

M let the enormity of that remark sink in as Miss Moneypenny handed her a file. M glanced at it, and then at Bond.

"I see the good doctor has cleared you," she said. "Notes you have 'exceptional stamina.' "

Moneypenny threw a look to Dr. Warmflash's skirt and saw that her slip was showing, slightly askew.

"I'm sure she was moved by his dedication," Moneypenny said brightly. "To the job at hand."

Dr. Warmflash picked up Moneypenny's gaze and quickly adjusted her skirt. Bond noted this and looked away.

"Thank you, Miss Moneypenny, Doctor," M said.

After the two ladies left the room, Bond asked, "Where is Double-O Nine? I'd like a word with him."

"He's in the Far East, on assignment. I assure you that anything he could tell you is in Renard's file. If only his aim had been a little better."

"And what about Double-0 Twelve?"

"As the case now appears to be related to Sir Robert's murder, I'll see that you get the file on that, too. Double-0 Seven, I want you to go to Elektra. She's taken over the construction of her father's oil pipeline from the Caspian Sea. Find out who switched that pin. If your instincts are right, Renard will be back—and Elektra is the next target."

"The worm on the hook again," Bond said. "Protect the girl, but kill Renard?"

M gave Bond a silent acknowledgment with her eyes that the latter deed was understood.

"Elektra doesn't need to know the same man may be after her. Don't frighten her."

"A shadow operation."

M narrowed her eyes at Bond. "Remember—shadows stay behind—or in front—but never on top."

She knew him all too well.

4

Blood and Oil

James Bond picked up the BMW Z8 in Turkey, then drove east until he came to the southern range of the Caucasus, which forms the border between Turkey and Iran, and the former Soviet satellites of Georgia, Armenia, and Azerbaijan. The gigantic snowcapped peak of the volcano Mount Aergius floated above a layer of clouds, an effect that was breathtaking.

The Z8 had evolved naturally from the legendary BMW 507. It had been shipped as promised by the overly efficient Q Branch Deputy (he also shipped the Aston Martin, as he was sure 007 would ultimately need a backup). A two-seater open sports car with a sleek engine compartment and streamlined body design, the Z8 came equipped with a six-speed transmission and a four-hundred-horsepower V-8 engine. Bond was so invigorated by the feel of its power that he had to remind himself continually to slow down.

After a while, the Z8 entered an area of desolate oil fields. The road snaked along an oil pipe that would ultimately lead Bond to his destination. He was all alone on the road, so he pushed the car to its limit. Still, he had a nagging feeling that he was being watched. He remained alert and vigilant, constantly checking his mirrors and heads-up display that would indicate the presence of other vehicles within a ten-mile radius. So far, though, he might as well have been the only person in the deserted valley.

The pipeline eventually moved into a dense, wooded area. The car roared through the pines, keeping with the oil pipe. It wouldn't be far now.

Suddenly an icon flashed on the display. There was an aircraft above him. Two minutes later, Bond could hear the sound of a helicopter. He looked out of the window and saw that it was a lifting aircraft, carrying a huge crate suspended beneath it. A King Industries logo was painted on the side of the crate.

The chopper passed Bond, moving ahead and beyond his vision. It was obviously headed for the construction site, too.

Still following the pipeline, Bond finally saw the end of the forest approaching. As the car emerged from the pines, a tiny speck on the vast landscape, Bond was fairly certain that his presence was already being announced by hidden guards, probably wearing forest camouflage.

The King Industries pipeline construction site was massive, teeming with ultramodern robotic machines and vehicles, as well as an airstrip. It was a huge undertaking. Sir Robert's intention was to open up a different oil pipeline to the west from the rich oil fields in the Caspian Sea. The project, which had already been running for a few years, had a long way to go. The difficult part would be digging through the mountains to the east and connecting with another part of the pipeline in Azerbaijan.

Bond pulled the BMW near the buildings marked as construction offices, and stopped. He got out, squinting into the bright sun. A slim man in his early thirties stepped out of the office and smiled.

"Can I help you?" he asked. He had an accent that was somewhere between Ukrainian and Muscovite.

"I'm looking for Elektra King," Bond said. He produced an ID card and showed it to the man. "My name is Bond. James Bond. Universal Exports."

The man took the card, glanced at it, and then held out his hand. "Sasha Davidov. Head of Security. Nice to meet you."

Bond shook his hand. The grip was firm. "And now you can call off the thugs standing behind me with the guns."

Davidov was impressed. He smiled again, then made a motion behind Bond. Sure enough, three construction workers shouldered weapons and moved away.

"Please don't call them thugs," Davidov said. "It upsets them."

The two men shared a laugh just as the high-pitched

whine of an executive helicopter filled the air.

"I know Miss King is expecting you."

The helicopter swooped in over the trees on its final approach. Bond put his hand to his brow. The scope of the site was staggering. Other helicopters were trailing giant saws that were cutting down trees to clear the pipeline right-of-way. Mammoth machines were dragging the trees away. It was a huge, awe-inspiring operation.

The lifting helicopter appeared overhead, still carrying the crate, and slowly descended. As soon as the crate touched the ground, workers moved in on it. A switch here, a lever there—and within moments, Bond could see that the object was, in fact, an expanding mobile office. The space within was increased by sliding the walls out, they operated much like filing-cabinet drawers. Just as a Citation landed on the runway in the distance, the mobile office had doubled its size and was ready for immediate operation.

Sasha Davidov and his men went into action as the jet taxied to a stop. Tense and alert, they drew their guns and scanned the perimeter. Bond joined in, falling easily into his job as Elektra King's protector. He still felt as if they were being watched, but everything looked clear.

"Have there been any threats?" Bond asked Davidov.

"No," the Head of Security said with tight lips. "We had a lot of trouble with sabotage for a long time. Not so much here, but in Azerbaijan. Here they just throw rocks. The countrymen in Azerbaijan blew up stuff. I guess they did not approve of a pipeline being constructed through their home. Sir Robert was very concerned about it. As far as he was concerned, they were terrorists. Miss King is more tolerant of their feelings. Anyway, I put in extra security. It seems to be all right now."

"But nothing here? Nothing recently?" Bond asked.

"No. But since . . . 'the incident' with Sir Robert, we all feel terrible . . . Responsible . . ."

"Because it happened on your watch?"

"Of course."

Across the tarmac, the plane stopped, the hatch opened, and the stairs swung down. The new CEO of King Industries stepped out, beautiful and elegant as ever. She was immediately surrounded by a phalanx of security guards. Not looking at Bond, she strode directly toward the mobile office and entered.

"Shall we?" Davidov asked Bond.

He followed the Ukrainian inside the fully functional office. Everything appeared to have been in use for weeks—computers, phones, a kitchen, and a wall map of the pipeline. Elektra was in the middle of a group of workmen, dressing down a foreman.

"Moustafa!" she said, using a teasing, warmly affectionate tone to express her displeasure. "You promised me that clearing would be finished last week. Are you telling me we're not going to meet my father's schedule?"

The foreman sheepishly replied, "We've had some trouble with the villagers at Ruan. Some sacred burial plot . . ."

She looked off, exasperated, noticing Davidov and Bond for the first time.

"Miss King?" Davidov interrupted. "Mr. Bond is here to see you."

She nodded, then returned to the foreman. "Find me the research on the limestone deposits, place these orders, bring me the budget reports, and get the Jeep ready. I'll deal with the problems at Ruan myself—"

Davidov interjected, "Miss King, I wouldn't recommend—"

"Sasha," she said, smiling at him indulgently. "I know what you would recommend. But I am going to Ruan. They're my mother's people. So prepare the Jeep." She addressed everyone else in the room. "And the rest of you—out. Get back to work while I deal with our mysterious guest."

Turning her back on Bond, she opened the door and held it for all of the men to file out. Watching this, Bond found himself intrigued by the woman. He liked her style, the easy way she flirted with the foreman yet got her instructions across. She was settling well into her role as boss.

"M told me she was sending someone," she said, closing the door and attempting to maintain the facade.

"She has great affection for you," Bond said.

"In many ways, she's like a mother to me." She paused, then said, "I saw you at my father's funeral."

"Yes. I'm sorry."

"Did you ever meet him?"

"Once. Briefly."

"It's funny . . . You go through an entire day and do not think about it. Then the tiniest thing—a sound, a smell—a stranger's face—and it all comes rushing back.

Have you ever lost a loved one, Mr. Bond?"

"James." He decided not to tell the whole truth. "I've had to give up loved ones."

He could feel her searching his face, trying to assess him. Bond did his best not to give anything away and pressed on. "M sent me because we're afraid you may be in danger."

She laughed scornfully, walked to the map on the wall, and said, "My father was murdered. I have a duty to fulfill the company's goals. I'm trying to finish building his oil pipeline—eight hundred miles of it. Through Turkey, bypassing Iraq, Iran, and Syria." She pointed to the map. "To the north, there are three competing Russian pipelines, and those people will do anything to stop me." She turned back to him. "And you—dear Mr. Bond—are here to tell me MI6 thinks I might be in danger?"

In the face of her ironic attack, Bond realized that he had to divulge more than he wished. "We think it might be an insider."

Before she could respond, there was a knock at the door. A large, imposing bodyguard popped his head in. His skin was black as coal and he wore his hair in dreadlocks.

"Excuse me, Miss King, the Jeep is ready," he said.

"Thank you," she said. The man's eyes went to Bond, then back to Elektra, before he closed the door.

"Someone close to me?" she asked. "Do you want to interrogate my bodyguard?"

"His name is Gabor," Bond said, referring to the man they had just seen. "He's from Fiji. A warrior—from

Beqa Island. He's been protecting you since the kidnapping."

Elektra's eyes flashed at the mention of the word "kidnapping." The stranger who was James Bond knew too much, and it angered her.

She turned, ready to walk out. "Mr. Bond, thank you for coming. But I already have a bodyguard—"

Bond grabbed her by the arm. "Elektra—" He pulled the burned lapel pin from his pocket and showed it to her.

"That was my father's . . ." she said, stunned. Tears welled in her eyes.

"No. A duplicate. With a receiver inside that set off the bomb. Someone in your organization switched the real one with this. I'm here to protect you . . . and find out who was responsible."

She pushed it away from her. "My family has relied on MI6 twice. I won't make that mistake a third time."

With that, she opened the office door and left the building. Bond followed her outside to a Jeep, where Gabor was holding the passenger door open for her. She turned and said, "Mr. Bond, I am going to finish building this pipeline. For my father, and for myself." She got in the Jeep and looked at a clipboard that was on the dash. "And I don't need your help. I hope you have a pleasant flight home."

But Bond had already slipped into the driver's seat. He reached over her lap and pulled the passenger door shut, leaving a befuddled Gabor standing outside the vehicle. Elektra looked at Bond, speechless.

"I thought I might visit Ruan on my way home," Bond said. "Buckle up. It's safer that way."

The Jeep took off before Elektra King could say a word.

They drove through the oil fields, a blighted, petrified forest of iron. Elektra gave the directions, but otherwise didn't say much. Attempting to break the ice, Bond commented, "I see we've taken the scenic route."

Slightly insulted, she asked, "Do you know what you're looking at? There was a time when this was the most coveted spot on earth."

Bond nodded. "Yes. I know. The oil fields here were discovered at the end of the last century. The Soviets seized them in 1919. Hitler wanted them. Stalin and Khrushchev used them to fuel the cold war."

She was impressed. "I see you've done your homework. But your treatise lacks passion."

Bond waited for her to explain.

"It was my mother's people who discovered this oil," she said. "The Bolsheviks slaughtered them for it. And when the Soviet Union fell, this was the legacy they left us. Some say the oil is in my family's blood. I say our blood is in the oil."

It wasn't long before they heard the sound of a helicopter above them. Bond looked up and saw a Eurocopter Dauphin with the King Industries logo on it. She said, "It's Gabor and Sasha. I'm sure they just want to keep tabs on me."

The Jeep passed from the derricks into a rock-strewn terrain. It was a moonscape not unlike the rocky deserts of Arizona in the United States, but with Stonehenge-like formations jutting out from the ground. They soon began to pass signs of civilization. Among groupings of curious "three-headed" fairy chimneys was a row of souvenir stalls.

Soon they were in the village of Ruan itself, which had once been a monastic retreat. The most striking points of interest, Bond noted, were the various churches and primitive cliff dwellings. Elektra explained that archaeologists had discovered cave paintings and other ancient artifacts in them.

"It's all prehistory, here. Noah's Ark supposedly wound up on one of the mountains not far away," she said.

They came to a break in the pipe along the road where King Industries had set up a survey camp. The Jeep appeared to have arrived just in time, for the survey crew were cowering behind a four-wheel-drive as men threw stones at them from a village carved into the rock. The people were shouting, ready to come out and storm the camp.

Before Bond could stop her, Elektra got out of the vehicle and moved to the crowd. The stoning suddenly ceased when the villagers saw her. They knew who she was. Bond watched protectively as she took a few of the leaders aside and spoke quietly to them in their tongue. After a moment, the crowd parted, making way for an Orthodox priest who motioned to her.

"Come."

She nodded and followed him through the crowd of tribesmen to a stunning Byzantine chapel hewn into the rock. Flames illuminated the mosaics and paintings on the walls. Bond stayed in the shadows, allowing Elektra to handle the situation. She was obviously quite capable of being an arbitrator. As she quietly talked with the priest, Bond stepped out and looked around. He noticed that Davidov's helicopter had landed nearby, and that he and the bodyguard were walking up to the chapel.

Why did he feel so edgy? It was an all-too-familiar feeling, and Bond was experienced enough to know that in this regard his sixth sense was rarely wrong. Someone was definitely watching them.

Davidov and Gabor were scanning the area, too.

"You had a good vantage point up there. See anything?" Bond asked.

Davidov shook his head. "No, I think we're all right." He shook his head in admiration. "She certainly has a way with the people. Much more so than her father ever had!"

"How well did Elektra get along with her father?"

"They fought all the time."

"Really?"

"Let's just say that they disagreed on business issues."

"Was Sir Robert well liked in the company?" Bond asked.

"No one had any problems with him, as far as I know. I've been with the company for seven years. He was a good employer and had innovative ideas. I think the only one who ever argued with him was his daughter."

"What's the general feeling in the company about the change in management?"

"Everyone loves Miss King. You've seen for yourself

how she deals with people. As for her management abilities, it's too early to tell for certain, but I think she'll be just fine."

Ten minutes later, Elektra and the priest emerged. The priest went to his people and led them away while Elektra, a determined look on her face, strode to the survey crew's foreman.

"Reroute the pipe around," she ordered.

"But it will take weeks, cost millions," he said. "Your father approved this route."

"Then my father was wrong," she said. "It is a sacred burial ground. We have to respect the wishes of the people."

"But—"

"Just do it."

The foreman was surprised. It was the first time Elektra had asserted her authority. He didn't question her.

She turned to Bond and said, "Well, Mr. Bond, you've seen Ruan. Now you can go home to London and report that I'm fine. Tell M not to worry. Now, if you'll excuse me, I have to check the upper lines."

"I've always wanted to see the upper lines," Bond said.

"Gabor will drive you back."

"Gabor can take care of himself."

She exchanged a look with Gabor. "So can I," she said.

"Then I'm sure Gabor won't mind."

She glanced at her bodyguard a second time. The man made a gesture to indicate that he wasn't offended.

"You don't take no for an answer, do you?" she asked Bond.

"No."

She sighed. "Look, I have to go up into the mountains. There's snow and ice up there, so I have to do this on skis."

"Sounds like fun," he said cheerfully.

At first she looked as if she might hit him, but then she reluctantly grinned out of the side of her mouth. "Come on," she said, gesturing toward the helicopter.

Bond's nagging feeling that they were being watched was not a product of his imagination. Had he or Sasha Davidov been able to peer into a clump of trees on a hill overlooking the village, they would have seen a man dressed in camouflage, perched on a branch, and equipped with a walkie-talkie.

Renard put a pair of binoculars to his eyes and watched the entourage prepare to leave Ruan.

Yes, there was the MI6 man, Bond. Renard had been correct in assuming that M would send him. This would be his day of reckoning . . .

His eyes focused on the girl for a moment. She looked as beautiful as ever. An image flashed into his brain— her tear-streaked face, her arms bound . . . Those eyes of hers . . . The silky-smooth skin . . . The memory was haunting, but Renard pushed it out of his mind and concentrated on the task at hand.

He waited until the Jeep pulled away toward the construction site, then he spoke into the walkie-talkie.

"Are they headed for the mountains?" he asked.

"Yes," came the reply.

"Then you know what to do. Proceed as planned. I'll be waiting for your report."

"Right."

"One other thing . . ." Renard paused for effect. "I want to see the snow up there covered in blood."

5
Snow Prey

The Dauphin swooped over the snowy wastes until it reached the mountain peak that Elektra indicated as their destination. The wind was buffeting the Eurocopter so violently that the pilot was having trouble navigating.

"Can't land!" he shouted. "Wind's too strong!"

"Hold her steady!" Elektra called back. She moved her goggles down onto her face. "We'll have to jump," she said to Bond. "You *do* ski, don't you?"

"Ladies first." Bond lowered his own goggles and put on the all-mountain-carving skis he had borrowed from Davidov. The security man's polypropylene jacket, fleece gloves, and ski pants with micro-fleece lining also happened to fit Bond. He slipped on the Q jacket over everything, glad that he had brought it along. Elektra wore a light parka jacket with a fur-lined hood and underarm zippers, down mittens, and ski pants similar to Bond's. She stepped into her all-mountain skis made especially for women, with a lightweight core and soft flex pattern. She fitted her boots into the toeholds and locked them down.

The cold wind rushed in when she opened the door. Without checking to see if Bond was ready, she leaped out and dropped fifteen feet, landing on the move. Bond jumped after her, but she was already way ahead. Her skiing was fearless.

Considering this a challenge, Bond went into the langlaufing method of sliding forward, something his old instructor, Fuchs, had taught him. It was exhilarating to be on skis once again. The only thing more thrilling than speeding down snow-covered slopes was skydiving. The rush of wind on his body was invigorating as he felt his adrenaline kick in. The skis were good ones: they had a turning radius of twenty-six meters. Two ribs ran the length of the skis to deliver good torsional properties. Bond considered it important to have an excellent front-to-back flex with minimal bending from side to side, plus a smooth feeling of stability.

He caught up with Elektra just as the slope leveled out. She pulled to the edge of a cliff and stopped cleanly. Bond arrived a moment behind her.

"Not bad," she said. "You ski very well, Mr. Bond."

"You seem to enjoy being chased. Probably happens all the time."

"Less often than you might think."

She pointed to the sparkling, white valley below. A line of survey flags ran down the middle.

"We're building from both ends," she said, a bit breathless. "Four hundred miles in that direction are the new oil fields in the Caspian Sea. Four hundred miles that way is the Mediterranean."

"So they meet here," Bond said, appreciating the strategy behind the company's plans.

"When the Persian Gulf and all the other oil fields have dried up, which *will* happen at the rate the world keeps increasing its demand for oil, this will once again be the heart of the earth. We'll still be pumping our lifeblood. And this will be the main artery."

"Your father's legacy?"

"My *family's* legacy. To the world."

They stood there a moment as she calculated distances in her head and studied the arrangement of survey flags. He watched her, admiring the determination and dedication she had for the work. He liked a girl who was passionate about her work and he had to resist the urge to take her in his arms.

Without warning, she pushed off with her sticks and soared down the slope toward the flags. Bond chuckled to himself. The girl really *did* like to be chased. He saw right through her. This was all for his benefit—a test, perhaps, to see what he was made of. Well, if it was a chase she wanted . . .

He pushed off and followed her, maneuvering easily between the survey markers. She zigzagged through them as if she were on a professional obstacle course. Bond mimicked her every move and stayed in perfect synchronization behind her. At one point, she leaped over a ridge, sailed through the air for twenty feet, and landed with the form of an Olympic champion. Bond went over the ridge with a little more speed than she did and almost spilled. He caught his balance as he landed, but he was thankful she hadn't seen the slightly awkward jump.

She had stopped again by another ridge. He pulled up beside her and stopped.

"You're not getting tired, are you?" she asked, peering out over another slope of survey markers.

"Not on your life," he replied. What a handful this girl was! He watched her as she studied the positions of the markers and made mental notes. What was especially attractive about her was the way she could appear aloof toward him, yet at the same time he could sense that she was constantly watching him out of the corner of her eye. Bond knew enough about women to glean that she was attempting to hide the fact that she was interested in him.

The sound above them interrupted his reverie. It was not the helicopter that had given them a lift. He looked up and saw four dark objects falling from the back of a Casa 212 airplane. As they plummeted silently toward the earth, parachutes popped open, slowing their descent. Elektra noticed them, too.

"Parahawks," she said. "Four men on Parahawks."

They were ingenious, deadly devices. "Parahawks" were essentially low-flying, sleek, all-terrain, all-season snowmobiles made with fully welded, lightweight, aircraft-grade aluminum frames. They came equipped with high-performance parachutes, handlebar steering, and thumb throttle control. The parachutes could be adjusted in-flight, allowing the pilots to vary speed by about five miles per hour. Powered by Rotax 582, sixty-five-horsepower engines with six-blade IVO props, the vehicles were able to fly, jump, and glide in an uncanny fashion.

Bond looked around for an escape route and noticed a ravine not too far down the mountain. The forest was in the opposite direction.

"Head for the gully. I'll lure them to the trees!" he said. He pulled his gun and pointed her off to one side. Elektra complied and skied away. Bond turned back to the sound of the approaching machines.

Suddenly gunfire blasted from the four terrifying shapes. He ducked, then streaked toward the woods as the vehicles shot after him in pursuit.

He assumed his old Alberg crouch, with hands forward of his boots, and headed downslope as the Parahawks gave chase. Bullets pockmarked the snow around him as he slalomed through the open area toward the trees below.

The noise suddenly grew louder. Bond ducked just as one of the Parahawks swooped low, trying to hit him. He retained the bulletlike stance, increasing his speed on top of the soft, powdery snow. He thought he was making some headway when the ground erupted in a terrible, deafening noise as he skied over it.

Now they were tossing hand grenades.

Bond performed a Sprung-Christiana, a showy turn that enabled him to swerve around and fire at the Parahawk. Unfortunately, the rounds bounced off the bullet-proofed vehicle.

Bond turned again, then slalomed into the forest, whipping in and out of the trees as two Parahawks followed. The gunfire continued, bullets hitting the snow frighteningly close to him.

One Parahawk took the lead, and in rapt concentration, the pilot attempted to fire at Bond from a different angle. The man was too close. Sooner or later he would get lucky.

The skis cut through the ice and snow, creating the high-pitched, scraping sound that in normal circumstances Bond would have considered music to his ears. Instead, he had to make sure that the sound was continuous and rhythmic, which indicated that he was not losing speed or breaking the pattern of his movements. At one point, the left ski thumped against a tree that came too close. Bond almost lost his balance but he was able to right himself on one ski and sail safely between two boulders and into another stretch of forest.

The lead Parahawk was gaining on him. Bond looked ahead at the terrain. He thought that if he could keep the Parahawk in the same position for a few more seconds, simple geometry and the law of gravity would take over and become his allies. Bond skied toward his goal and turned sharply at the precise moment.

The Parahawk whisked past a large tree, but the parachute caught in its branches, causing the machine to catapult backward into the tree. The vehicle exploded with tremendous force.

Elektra, having made it safely through the gully,

stopped at the sound of the explosion. Where was Bond? She peered over the tops of the trees and saw two of the Parahawks still sailing through the air. Should she stay put? Her better judgment told her to wait it out, but she was a stubborn girl. Elektra threw caution to the winds and decided to ski onward in Bond's direction.

Meanwhile the second Parahawk and a third one continued the pursuit. Bond soared evasively through the trees as grenades were tossed right and left. Then the two vehicles ejected their chutes and hit the ground moving. Without missing a beat, the drivers continued to rip up the snow around Bond with machine guns.

He skied into a clearing, possibly the worst place he could go. He prepared to push with his sticks and increase speed, but realized that he could no longer hear the sound of the Parahawks' motors. Glancing behind him, he saw that the vehicles had disappeared. What the . . . ?

Bond didn't alter his speed. He headed for the opposite edge of the clearing, then slid into the woods once again. Had he succeeded in losing them so quickly?

He had barely formulated the question when the two Parahawks erupted into view, scaring the hell out of him. Bond felt the heat of two bullets whiz just past his face as the gunfire assailed him. The last Parahawk joined them, higher up, and continued to drop grenades.

The Parahawk nearest to him moved ahead so that the pilot could swing around and come at Bond from the front. It headed straight for him, gun barrel aimed for the center of Bond's body.

Bond saw his assailant just in time and made a split-second decision that there was only one thing to do. He continued on, directly toward the Parahawk, in a seemingly suicidal, head-on move. The pilot's eyes widened as Bond approached at an overwhelming speed. Then Bond hit a snowbank in front of the Parahawk, and leaped over the craft as the pilot opened fire. Bond landed safely on the other side, but the pilot lost control of the vehicle. He smashed into a tree, once again rocking the terrain with a deafening explosion. A fire spread quickly through the trees, creating a wall between Bond and the other Parahawk.

Two down, two to go. Bond took stock of the situation. One of them was high above him, throwing grenades. Had the wall of flames stopped the other one? He turned to look.

The Parahawk burst through the fire, unharmed, spraying gunfire. Bond skied on, harder, expertly maneuvering in and out of the trees. This couldn't go on much longer, he thought. The skier's weak point, the knees, were becoming unbearably sore. He set his jaw and pushed on, avoiding the grenades which, unfortunately, were being dropped more precisely.

He almost didn't see the precipice. He came upon it suddenly and dropped parallel with the ground in an attempt to skid to a stop before plummeting off. He slid fifteen feet farther than he had intended, but managed to break his fall against a tree stump. The Parahawk's pilot, however, wasn't so lucky. Unable to stop in time, the vehicle flew over Bond and off the edge into what appeared to be a five-hundred-foot-deep abyss.

"See you back at the lodge," Bond said, under his breath.

His regained confidence was, however, suddenly deflated as he watched the falling Parahawk deploy an emergency parachute from the back. The pilot performed a climbing turn, joined the other remaining Parahawk, and headed straight back toward Bond.

He got up and went back in the direction that he had come, then took a different path along the edge of the cliff. The Parahawks were hot on his tail. Bond skied for his life toward what looked like some kind of ice bridge that spanned the chasm. One pilot saw it, too, and directed his vehicle over the yawning space so that he could swoop down lower than Bond and come up on the other side. The other pilot circled around the other way so that he could assault him from the opposite direction. Bond would be sandwiched in, with nowhere to go.

The only way out was to perform a very risky move, so he did what the pilot least expected him to do. Instead of using the ice bridge to cross the abyss, Bond turned abruptly and jumped across the chasm just as the Parahawk was beside him in midair. Bond's skis slashed through the top of the parachute, ripping it to shreds. He landed upright on the other side of the precipice and kept going.

The disabled Parahawk was out of control. It wobbled in the air precariously, sailing with great speed right into . . . the other Parahawk. The two vehicles burst into flames, sending a thunderclap in all directions.

Bond slowed to a stop and caught his breath. That

had been much too close. Where was Elektra? Had she made it through that gully safe and sound? And where the hell were her bodyguards? They were supposed to have been keeping watch.

Elektra found him before he could move. She glided to him from the ice bridge and stopped at his side. Another explosion from the burning Parahawks rocked the ground. She fell into his arms and, surprisingly, allowed him to protect her.

"Are they gone? All of them?" she asked, quite frightened. Her earlier bravado was missing.

"I think so," he said.

"I couldn't wait for you up there. I decided to come downhill and catch up with you at the bottom."

"It was probably a good thing that you did, otherwise I might never had found you," he said. "All I need is to get lost in the Caucasus Mountains."

He looked down and saw that a small piece of parachute fabric was stuck to his right ski. There was some kind of pattern on it. He reached down and slid the fabric off, then frowned when he saw the Russian letters sewn onto the cloth: the logo of the Russian Atomic Energy Department.

Bond stuffed the Russian-made piece of parachute into his pocket just as they heard a low rumbling around them.

"What was that?" she asked.

The noise grew louder. Bond looked up the hill and saw that the exploding Parahawks had triggered a collapse of the overhanging snow. A huge, white wall was tumbling toward them.

"Come on!" he cried. He was ready to keep skiing, for the best strategy to avoid an oncoming avalanche is to point one's skis downhill and simply outrace it.

Elektra, however, lost her balance and fell. Bond stopped and threw his body on top of hers.

"Curl up into a ball!" he shouted. It was the only possible defense. If the hands were near the feet, a person could unlock the boots, slowly unfold, and burrow oneself out of the snow.

The avalanche hit them hard just as Bond pulled the toggle on his Q jacket. The air bag slammed open, forming a cushion between Elektra and him and the snow. The cold weight engulfed their bodies, and for a moment everything went dark. She screamed and started to panic. Bond held her tightly, forcing her to stay still.

"It's all right . . . shhh . . ." he whispered to her. Finally, after what seemed to be an eternity, everything went dead. The only relief from the blackness was the faint illumination of Bond's watch. He unlocked the toeholds and pushed his skis away, trying to straighten himself. He was able to grab the Sykes-Fairbairn throwing knife from the sheath on his calf, then reach around and puncture the air bag. Once it had deflated, they were left inside a small, igloolike, icy tomb. They were safe, but they were trapped.

"My God, we've been buried alive," Elektra gasped.

"We're all right," he said.

She started to panic again. "I can't stay here."

"You're not going to." He used the knife to start chipping away at the snow above them.

"No! It will cave in!"

"It's the only way out . . ."

"Oh God, oh God," she cried. She started breathing rapidly, hyperventilating. It was obvious that she was having an attack of claustrophobia.

"Hold on, Elektra, I'll get us out," Bond said, working feverishly with the knife.

"I can't breathe . . . I can't breathe . . ." she choked.

Bond stopped and grabbed her.

"Elektra! Look at me!" She struggled against him. "Look in my eyes!" She continued to beat at him until he slapped her lightly on the cheek. Then she stopped and gasped a lungful of air.

"You're all right," he said gently. "Everything will be all right. Trust me."

Finally, arrested by the strength in his eyes and the shock of the blow, Elektra calmed down and nodded. He continued to chip away.

Bond now understood the girl better. The kidnapping ordeal had been much harder on her than she liked to admit, he thought. But she was on the right track. Given her situation, the best thing would be to do everything within her power to put the experience behind her and move forward. Immerse herself in work. And she had done that, most admirably, but the scars still remained, hidden and unhealed wounds to her psyche. Knowing this, Bond guessed that Elektra had probably developed the claustrophobia within the past year, and with this thought he began to appreciate the amount of stress she was under. Not enough time had passed for her to recover from the kidnapping, and then suddenly her father is murdered, and she finds herself in the position of having to take charge of the pipeline project. . . . It was no wonder that she seemed to be walking a fine line between composure and sheer panic. M had been right to send him out to protect her. He resolved to be doubly careful not to let her know that Renard was still after her.

Six minutes later, Bond's fist broke through the mound that covered them. He enlarged the hole with his arms and pulled himself up and out. He then reached down and helped Elektra.

As if on cue, the Dauphin appeared overhead.

"It's Sasha!" she cried, waving.

With rescue imminent, the ordeal was in effect, over, and Elektra smoothly resumed the persona of a woman in charge. The cowering, frightened figure of only moments before had disappeared. She immediately began to babble about the survey markers and how she needed to get on to someone about moving some of them.

Bond found her transformation extraordinary. He admired her will to overcome her problems.

The helicopter circled around and found a clear area. Sasha dropped a rope ladder, and they trudged through the snow toward it. Neither Bond nor Elektra seemed any the worse for wear, but Bond knew that something had happened between them. She had changed. Elektra had shown him her vulnerable side and let down her tough, authoritative exterior.

He found her damnably attractive.

She had let him see through the facade. Would this make his assignment easier . . . or all the more difficult?

6
Baku

The major petroleum sources of Azerbaijan are located in the eastern and southeastern regions of the country, near the capital city of Baku, in the Caspian Sea, close to the border with Iran. Not long after Azerbaijan's formal declaration of independence, the country's government signed a production-sharing contract with a consortium of eleven international oil companies for the development of several deep-water oil fields in the Caspian. The deal provided the struggling country with much-needed capital to finance an infrastructure, which was, at best, fragile.

Freedom from Soviet control had promised a brighter future for the former republics in the region, including Georgia and Armenia, but violent conflict between various ethnic groups had been stifling progress. Foreign investment in anything other than oil was not forthcoming. Nevertheless, Baku had managed to become a major cultural and educational center. The largest city in the region, with a population of over a million people, its development was bolstered by the rapid growth of the petroleum industry. The influx of money in the area also brought free enterprise in the form of organized crime. SIS had known for some time that the so-called Russian Mafia was operating out of Baku. In many ways, the city is to southwestern Asia what Tangier was to the Mediterranean during World War II. In just a few years, it has become a haven for spies, drug smugglers, arms dealers, and other forms of lowlife.

This situation, however, had not stopped Sir Robert King from developing his interests in the Caspian Sea. King Industries moved in shortly after the country gained its independence, and the company was surprisingly successful at locating and finding the richest oil fields. Flush with his success, King built an ornate villa on the shore of the sea, some twenty miles south of Baku, where he and his family could stay when they were in the country.

This is where the King Industries entourage went the morning after the attempt on Elektra and Bond's lives. Elektra insisted that the work must go on, so Sasha Davidov and Gabor organized the trek across Georgia and Armenia into Azerbaijan. Elektra, of course, flew in her private jet. Bond drove the BMW east, over the mountains, with Gabor driving a careful distance behind him.

During the trip, Bond pondered the situation and the

events that had transpired on the mountains. Renard the Fox was assuredly the man behind the attack. It had been an expensive, daring operation, and one that only a man of his means and connections with Russian agencies could have organized. There was no question that Renard wasn't sparing any expense to see Elektra King . . . and him . . . dead.

Bond didn't enjoy dangling the bait in front of such a killer. Elektra, for all her bravado and stubbornness, was still very much a victim in the whole mess. She was a bird with a wing down, albeit a majestic one; and Bond found her irresistible. The side of the girl that he had seen when they were buried in snow was probably something few people ever witnessed. She knew it, too. It would be interesting to see how their relationship progressed.

The sun was setting and the sea was calm and quiet when he arrived at the villa, where he noticed gun-toting security men roaming the perimeter, their watchful eyes patrolling the roads for anything suspicious. Dead tired, he walked in on an argument between Elektra and her Head of Security. It seemed that Davidov was furious at Elektra for putting herself in danger on the mountains, but there was not much he could do about it. Once the oil heiress was back in the safe confines of her role as CEO, she had reassumed her authority. Bond knew, though, that underneath it all, Elektra was scared.

After she had refused to eat dinner, Davidov insisted that a doctor examine her. Bond waited with him and Gabor in the villa's drawing room while the patient was seen upstairs in her room.

"I still don't understand how we could have lost you," Davidov said, pacing the floor. "One minute you were at the top of the mountain, the next—"

"You found us, that's what matters," Bond said, sitting in a large wooden chair and nursing a glass of bourbon. He was exhausted. The meal of beef Wellington, new potatoes, asparagus, and beets, although delicious, had done little to recharge his batteries. He had to will himself to get a second wind soon, for he was not going to sit idle that night. Bond knew people in Baku.

"I still think we should have gone after that plane," Gabor said.

"The first priority was Elektra," Davidov said.

"I have an idea where we might find some answers," Bond said.

"Oh?" Davidov asked. "Are we going hunting?"

"*We* aren't. This is something I have to do alone."

They heard a door close upstairs, followed by footsteps. The doctor, a rather large man of Armenian heritage, waddled down the circular stairway that dominated the room.

Davidov looked at him expectantly.

"She's fine," the doctor said. "Some cuts and bruises, but otherwise fine." He gestured toward the men. "She wants to see you."

Davidov bolted for the stairs, but the doctor stopped him. "No, not you." He pointed at Bond. "Him."

Bond and Davidov shared a look, then Bond pulled himself out of the chair and walked up the stairs.

When he arrived in Elektra's ornate bedroom, the young woman was sitting near a window, looking at the sunset over the sea. She was dressed in a thin lace night-gown. Bond closed the door and walked over to her.

"Are you all right?"

"I need to ask you something," she said. "And I want you to tell me the truth. Who is it? Who's trying to kill me?"

Bond didn't want to get into this. "I told you. I don't know. But I'm going to find him—"

"That's not good enough," she said. Bond struggled with the desire to take her in his arms, tell her every-thing . . .

She turned to the window again and said, "After the kidnapping, I was afraid. Afraid to go outside, afraid to be alone, afraid to be in a crowd . . . afraid to do any-thing at all, until I realized . . ." She turned back to face him. There were tears in her eyes. "I realized I can't hide in the shadows. I can't let fear run my life. I *won't*."

Bond moved closer to her and hesitantly touched her shoulders. "After I find him, you won't have to. Now listen to me. I'm going to a casino in Baku tonight to speak with some . . . friends. I have an idea they might know where he is. I want you to stay put. You're safe here."

She looked up to him, her eyes pleading. He could read exactly what she wanted. "Don't go," she whis-pered. "Stay with me."

Her hand came up to caress his cheek. Bond looked from her hand to her face and saw the hint of promise and passion. He wanted her badly.

"Please . . ."

Bond slowly removed her hand. "I can't."

"I thought it was your job to protect me," she said.

"You'll be safe here."

"I don't want to be safe!" she said fiercely. She moved away from him, stinging from the rejection. Bond could see that Elektra King was a girl who was quite used to getting what she wanted, and didn't like it if she didn't.

Bond looked at his watch. If he was going to go, he needed to get moving.

"I'll be back as soon as I can." He strode toward the door and opened it.

"Who's afraid now, Mr. Bond?" she asked, under her breath but loud enough for him to hear. He stopped.

Was she right? Was he afraid of what he might feel if he gave in to his desire for her?

Without looking back at her, Bond coldly headed out the door.

The Casino l'Or Noir was a kind of living symbol of the elegant and mysterious world that Baku had become. Since the collapse of the Soviet Union, the city had metamorphosed from a simple industrial port to a modern-day equivalent of the long-gone international centers of intrigue, exotic places like Tangier or Casablanca, Macau, or old Hong Kong. SIS estimated that more than half of Azerbaijan's illegal activities originated in Baku's nightspots, of which the new casino was the most popular and well attended. The city's shadow figures gathered there at night, deals were made in back rooms while money was won and lost in public. The wealthy liked to be seen there, as it was *the* place for the powerful and beautiful in this part of the world.

James Bond wore a sharp Brioni tuxedo and Q's X-ray sunglasses, with which he could clearly make out every concealed weapon in the room. All sizes of pistols were underneath jackets, even the odd grenade. As an added, if not fully intended, bonus, the glasses also allowed Bond to see through clothes.

He walked around the perimeter of the main room until he found the curtained-off alcove he was looking for. Two beautiful women crossed in front of him before he could enter. One turned back to look at him and smile, unaware that she was totally on display. Her friend turned to look at Bond, too. He smiled back, nodding hello. The second woman had a pistol concealed in her bra.

Bond slipped through the curtains and found a small, private bar where a bartender was chopping ice with a pick in the sink under the counter. A large thug in a suit and tie sat on a stool across from him. Through the X-ray glasses, Bond could see that the man was a walking arsenal—guns, knives, and a cudgel were all contained within his jacket. He was Bond's kind of guy.

He walked up to the man and stood next to the bar. Nonchalantly, he said, "I want to see Valentin Zukovsky."

The thug took a sip from his drink but didn't look up. Then, turning menacingly to Bond, he said, "This is a private bar. There is no Zukovsky here. So hit the road."

"Tell him James Bond is here."

The thug blinked, leaned forward, started to stand and reach into his jacket for a gun. "I said, *this is a private bar*. Do I have to escort you—"

In one swift move, Bond grabbed the ice pick from the bartender, slammed it into the bar through the tip of the thug's tie, and kicked the stool out from under him. The brute fell and hung from the bar, gasping, strangled by his own tie. Bond reached inside the man's jacket, took the gun, and placed it on the bar.

"He tied one on," Bond said to the bartender.

Just then a hand twice as large as the thug's appeared and squeezed Bond's right shoulder. Bond turned and was confronted by a seven-foot-tall, light-skinned muscular man.

"Mr. Zukovsky will be *delighted* to see you," he said. The man's mouth was full of gold teeth. Bond recognized him immediately. Maurice Womasa, aka "The Bull" aka "Mr. Bullion"—hence, the teeth. A killer from Somalia, The Bull was wanted for genocide, among other unsavory acts.

Bond smiled, removed his glasses, and motioned to the door. "After you . . ."

"I insist," the big guy said, shaking his head.

"Of course you do." They left together through a door at the side of the bar. When they were gone, the half-strangled thug stood up and pulled the ice pick out of the bar, freeing himself. He placed the stool upright and sat down.

"Tourists . . ." he grumbled. The bartender refilled his glass and commiserated with him.

Bond hadn't seen Valentin Zukovsky since the GoldenEye affair a few years earlier. An ex-KGB official, Zukovsky had made a name for himself as a "freelancer," mainly in the Russian Mafia, although he refused to call it that. Bond had had a run-in with him before the fall of the Soviet Empire, giving the man his now-famous limp. Since then, the two men had reluctantly performed favors for one another almost as if competing to keep the other in debt.

Bond found Zukovsky sitting with two gorgeous women on his lap. He was spoon-feeding them caviar. He was as elephantine as ever, and his moon face was red from alcohol and the attention he was getting from the girls.

"BondJamesBond!" he said heartily. "Do come in! Meet Nina and Verushka."

"Lose the girls, Valentin," Bond said. He knew that he had to play it tough with Zukovsky, or else he'd never get anything out of him. He gestured toward The Bull. "And the toy bodyguard, too. We need to talk."

The big man grunted.

"Why am I suddenly worried I'm not carrying enough insurance?" Zukovsky asked. "Chill out. Try your luck in my new casino."

"Only if you're willing to place a bet on your knee— the one I didn't shoot out."

Zukovsky addressed the girls on his lap. "Do you see what I have to put up with? I'm out of the KGB ten years and—"

But a cold, no-nonsense look from Bond stopped him.

Bond drew his gun and aimed for Zukovsky's leg. "How *is* your knee? The good one, that is . . ."

The Bull drew his gun and aimed it at Bond's head. Bond held his ground.

Finally, the Russian sighed loudly. "Okay, ladies.

Scram. Beat it. I have business. It's all right, Maurice."

"But, Valentin," one of the girls whined. "You promised we could play!"

Zukovsky gestured to the big man. "Bull, give them an inch."

The bodyguard peeled off a wad of cash and held it high. The two girls leaped off of Zukovsky's lap and jumped for the money like trained seals. They snatched it, squealed, and ran out of the room.

"And make sure they lose it in *this* casino!" Zukovsky said to The Bull, who moved toward the door to keep watch on the girls. He turned back, smiling broadly to reveal the sparkling gold teeth.

"I will see you later, Mr. Bond."

"I can see you put your money where your mouth is," Bond said. The Bull flexed, ready to fight again, but Zukovsky waved him off.

"Mr. Bullion doesn't trust banks," he said. "It's all right, Maurice." The Bull made a face and left them alone. Bond holstered his gun.

"You have to excuse The Bull. He's my chauffeur and . . ." Zukovsky said, shrugging his stocky shoulders.

"Yes. I know all about Maurice Womasa. Crushes men with his bare arms and gives them a bright smile at the same time. Not to be confused with the other wild beasts and upstanding citizens floating through your casino—the Russian Mafia, Chinese gangsters, Turkish warlords—"

"*And* diplomats, bankers, oil executives, and anyone else who wants to do business in Baku." Zukovsky turned to the table and spooned some caviar onto a small plate. "I'm sorry to disappoint you, Double-0 Seven, but I'm a legitimate businessman now. Care for some caviar? My own brand. Zukovsky's finest."

"I want some information. About Renard."

Zukovsky frowned. "Renard? Renard the Fox?"

"How does a terrorist like Renard get his hands on the latest Russian military equipment? State-of-the-art Parahawks?"

Zukovsky shook his head. "That is not possible."

Bond produced the shred of parachute and showed it to him. "I think you know the characters. It's the Russian Special Services Division of the Atomic Weapons Branch."

"The Russian Atomic Energy Department. Where did you get this?" Zukovsky asked, genuinely curious about the fabric.

"Off a Parahawk that was trying to kill Elektra King this afternoon. I want to know if Renard has an insider . . . who sold the weapons . . . or if the Russian government itself wants her pipeline stopped. And I want to find Renard before he gets another chance to kill her."

Zukovsky glanced over Bond's shoulder and started to chuckle.

"What's so funny?" Bond asked.

"Nothing . . . Except it would appear Miss King does not share your concern."

Bond turned around to see a video monitor that was focused on the front doors of the casino. Elektra King had just entered.

She looked more vibrant and glamorous than Bond had ever seen her. She wore a sparkling dress that fit like a second skin, her hair was full and tumbling, and her eyes were fiery and wild.

The two men agreed to continue their conversation later. Bond left the alcove and returned to the main gambling hall. When she saw him approach, Elektra turned away defiantly, making her way to the blackjack tables. Bond followed her, and she moved away from him, catlike, through the neon jungle. The energy and noise of the place accentuated her own intensity as she passed the "Minimum $100" table, then $500, then $1000 . . . She finally stopped at the "No Limit" table, which was crowded with the nastiest and richest of the high rollers: Armenians, Turks, South Americans, Chinese, an American computer nerd, and a Russian industrialist's wife, heavy with jewelry and drink.

Zukovsky appeared and pulled out the center seat for Elektra. "Miss King. So nice to see you. We've kept your father's chair free."

"And his account?" she asked.

"A million, U.S. dollars. As always."

A pit boss materialized with a chit. She signed it with a flourish as a waitress took her order.

"Vodka martini," she said.

She was surprised to hear Bond's voice beside her. "Two. Shaken, not stirred."

As twenty $50,000 plaques were placed in front of her, Bond leaned in, smiling.

"What are you doing here?" he asked.

She smiled right back at him. "If someone wants to kill me, I'd rather die looking them straight in the eye. Whoever was responsible for the attack on that mountain is surely watching. I want to show them that I'm not afraid. What's your excuse? Wasn't I enough of a challenge?"

"If this little show is for my benefit, I'll take you home right now."

"You had your chance, James. But you played it safe." She turned to the dealer. "I'm ready. Deal." And, back to Bond: "You passed up a sure thing."

She tossed two $50,000 plaques onto the felt; the whole table reacted. Energized gamblers placed bets and the dealer dealt the cards.

Fine, Bond thought. *We'll play it her way.* She was terribly wound up and needed a release of some kind. Perhaps a public catharsis at the gambling table would do her good.

"Personally, I like to get a feel for the game—what the other players are holding—before I commit anything," Bond said, lightening up. He had to admit that the scent and smoke and sweat that were a part of all casinos everywhere excited him. He was curious to see how Elektra would handle winning and losing.

"Then maybe I should let *you* play the first hand this time," she said, smiling now. "I don't know how to play anyway. Perhaps you'd be more daring holding my fate in your hands. Come on, Mr. Bond, show me how it's done."

She looked him straight in the eye and licked the edges of her front teeth.

"All right," he said, giving in to her beauty and audacity.

Elektra had a black king showing and a four underneath. The dealer had a king showing.

"Do we stand? Or do we play?" she asked him.

"Card," Bond said to the dealer.

The dealer dealt them a seven.

"Twenty-one," the dealer announced. Bond and Elektra looked at each other triumphantly as the two other players passed. The dealer turned over his second card—an eight.

"Eighteen," the dealer said. "Miss King wins."

"Shall we raise the stakes?" she asked.

"It's your game," Bond said. She was positively luminous.

"Again," she said to the dealer. She pushed more plaques onto the table.

They called it the "Field of Fire."

Some ten miles outside of Baku, in the middle of a petroleum field, a Land Rover bearing the Russian Atomic Energy logo pulled to a stop at the top of a hill overlooking the eerie, hellish landscape. Natural gas seeped from holes in the baked earth, creating a gigantic, perpetual inferno. Against the night sky, the sight was like looking into a gas furnace that covered an area of half a mile square.

"We're here, Arkov."

Sasha Davidov got out of the Land Rover with another man in his sixties. Arkov wore the Russian emblem on a photo ID attached to his overalls.

"I'm telling you I have reservations now," Arkov said in a thick Russian accent. "I wouldn't be doing this if my pension was halfway decent. You're lucky you found someone in our organization that was willing to help. But how I will explain about the Parahawks, I don't know. This is crazy."

"Shut up," Davidov said, looking about. "Where the hell is he?"

The men stepped onto the hill and gazed at the field of flame, unsettled by the sound of hissing gas. They felt entirely alone and helpless, until . . .

"Welcome to 'The Devil's Breath,' gentlemen," came the familiar voice behind them. Davidov turned to see Renard and an armed bodyguard step into the light. The flickering from the flames cast bizarre patterns on Renard's bald head. The corner of his mouth on the bad side of his face turned down in an unintentional sneer. While his left eye blinked, the other one stayed open, frozen and eerie. Looking at Renard always gave Davidov the creeps.

"For thousands of years, Hindu pilgrims have journeyed to this holy place," Renard said, his voice full of awe and respect. "To witness the miracle of the natural flames that have never been extinguished . . . And to test their devotion to God by holding the scalding rocks in their hands as they said their daily prayers."

Renard squatted and picked up one of the rocks from the fire. It sizzled in his hand. The flesh began to smoke, but Renard showed no emotion. He tossed it up and down, like a baseball, then moved to Davidov.

"Tell me, Davidov. What happened on the mountains? You promised me your best men. Mr. Arkov here supplied the latest weaponry . . ."

"But Bond—" Davidov began.

"Was armed with . . . a pistol." Disgusted, Renard nodded to the bodyguard, who put his gun to the base of Davidov's skull.

"I'm becoming just a little annoyed with these MI6 agents who keep interfering with my plans. And you, Mr. Arkov," Renard asked, "is everything ready for tomorrow?"

"I have the authorizations and passes in the car," Arkov said. "And I've arranged for a plane tonight. But—"

"But what?"

"I think we should scrub the mission. I only borrowed the Parahawks. They were meant to be returned. They'll be asking questions, even of me." Arkov indicated Davidov. "Because of *his* screwup—his incompetence—it's too risky now. We're bound to be caught. I have no faith that the mission is foolproof."

Renard stepped to Davidov and looked at him, face-to-face.

"I see," he said. "You're right, Arkov. He *should* be punished." Renard stared into the frightened man's eyes. "Davidov, hold this for me." He shoved the burning stone into Davidov's hand and held it there. The man screamed in pain.

"It was wrong of me to expect so much of you," Renard said, relishing Davidov's agony. He nodded to the gunman. "Kill him."

But instead of shooting Davidov, the gunman quickly swung the pistol to Arkov and fired. The older man's head exploded and his body slumped to the ground.

"He failed his test of devotion," Renard said. He took

the stone away from the whimpering Davidov, then tossed it from hand to hand again without even flinching. It was curious—every day he felt less and less sensation. He almost wished that he *could* feel the pain and torture of the heat. Anything would be better than . . . nothing.

With sudden rage, Renard threw the stone as hard and as far as he could out into the burning field. He calmed down just as quickly and turned back to Davidov.

"There, there," Renard said, patting the man on the shoulder. "You'll take his place. Take his ID. And *do* be on time."

Davidov could only nod yes. He closed his eyes and dropped his head. He forced himself to open his eyes and examine his hand. It was seared, red and black.

A moment later, when he looked up, he was all alone—just himself, Arkov's body, and the Land Rover.

7

Pillow Talk and Passion

T here were now two stacks of twenty $50,000 plaques on the table. The other players had quit, save for Elektra and Bond, but a large group of people was watching the charismatic couple. Whether it was their luck, a concept that Bond refused to take seriously, or the chemistry between the two players that attracted the audience, no one could say. The excitement of the game had brought the couple cheek to cheek, and the crowd could sense sex in the air.

Valentin Zukovsky stood nearby, a frown on his face. He took some comfort in the fact that the girl had distracted Bond from asking him questions. The Bull draped himself beside a neighboring, unused blackjack table and watched with a detached, amused expression.

He made a point, though, of sneering whenever his eyes met Bond's. Gabor had also become curious and left his post at the front door to watch the game unfold.

The game continued as the dealer dealt a king and a four to Elektra and Bond. He had an eight showing. Elektra signaled for another card, which was a two. She hesitated, but Bond squeezed her waist gently, refuting his own rule to stand on sixteen or higher.

"Another, please," she said. The dealer turned over a three.

"Nineteen," he said.

Elektra stayed, and the dealer revealed his other card. A ten. They had won again.

She pushed another plaque onto the playing field and was dealt an ace and a jack—blackjack.

"Miss King is the winner," the dealer announced.

"Shouldn't we—?" Bond asked.

"Let's keep going," she said. "We're on a roll, wouldn't you say?" She threw another plaque on the table and nodded to the dealer.

He dealt a six and a nine to them.

"The player has fifteen," the dealer said, revealing his own ten. Elektra almost gestured that they would stay, but Bond placed his hand over hers and motioned for a card. It was a five.

"Twenty," the dealer said.

The crowd held its breath as the dealer revealed his second card. A nine.

"Nineteen," the dealer announced. "Miss King wins again." There were murmurs around the table. Zukovsky popped two chewable antacid tablets into his mouth.

Elektra turned to Bond with desire in her eyes and said, "You seem to have an unusually lucky touch—"

"With the cards," he interjected. "But I think it's time to call it a night."

"I prefer to press my luck." She looked at Zukovsky. "How much are we ahead?"

"Mr. Bond has doubled your initial investment," Zukovsky said unhappily.

"Then we'll play one more game. How about double or nothing?" she suggested. "One card, high draw?"

The crowd gasped at the audacity. She might as well just flip a coin.

"Elektra," Bond said gently. "Why not pay off your chit, and play with the winnings?"

"I thought you'd understand by now," she said, looking at him hard. "For me, there's no point in living unless I can feel alive."

"I'll take the bet," Zukovsky said. He put Elektra's million-dollar chit on the table, then pushed the dealer aside. "And I'll deal."

She smiled. The Russian turned the card shoe toward her. Elektra patted it for good luck and drew a card. Zukovsky pulled the shoe back and drew his own. She turned hers over. King of hearts.

"How appropriate," Bond said.

Zukovsky flipped his card. The ace of clubs.

He smiled. "It seems I've beaten you with an ace of clubs."

"How unsurprising," Bond said.

One of the dealers removed all her plaques as Zukovsky made a show of folding up her chit and putting it in his pocket.

"Perhaps you'll be luckier in love, my dear," he said. The crowd reacted noisily to that.

"Perhaps I will," Elektra said. "Enjoy your winnings."

She stood, dignified in defeat. "Shall we?" she asked Bond.

"Not your lucky night," he said, taking her arm and walking her toward the door. There was something strange about the exchange he had just witnessed, but he couldn't put his finger on what it was.

"Who said it was over?" she dared him.

Gabor was waiting for them near the front. He followed them outside and the three of them stood on the steps, waiting for the valet to bring Bond's car.

"What happened to Davidov?" Bond asked.

"I gave him the night off," Elektra said.

"And where in Baku would a man like Sasha Davidov go for fun on a night off?"

"I have no idea."

Bond thought it might be wise to find out. He was fairly certain that whoever the traitor was, he was very close to, if not part of, the King Industries inner circle. Perhaps he ought to have a look in the security office when he had the chance.

Neither Bond nor Gabor could see the two men on the roof of the opposite building. There was absolutely no illumination there, and they were dressed in black. One of them had a high-powered FN FAL sniper rifle. He had it trained on Bond and waited for the signal.

When it didn't come, he asked the other man, "What about Bond? Sir?"

Renard, looking through binoculars, was mesmerized by the sight of Bond's hand on the small of Elektra's back. Watching their confident sensuality made him terribly ill at ease, but it gave him an idea. It meant a change of plans. Renard placed a hand on the gunman's shoulder, indicating that he should relax.

"Not now, my friend," he said.

Although the Syrian doctor had told him that he would feel nothing in the head wound, Renard often felt the bullet moving. He had come to think of it as a living thing with a mind of its own. He felt it now, throbbing, anxious to burrow itself further into his brains, like an earwig might tunnel through the soft tissues of the head and lay its eggs along the way. Renard put a hand to the fleshy mound at his temple and rubbed it. He couldn't feel any sensation there.

The gunman removed the sight and stock from the gun when they saw the BMW pull around to the front of the casino. Renard watched intently as Bond held the passenger door open for Elektra.

Once again, the girl's beauty affected him in ways he could not predict. Renard experienced a wave of confusing emotions—jealousy, desire . . .

The memory flashed into his head once more: the lovely young girl, bound in front of him, helpless . . . her skin, so soft . . .

"Sir?"

Renard caught himself. "What?"

"You said something."

Had he been talking to himself?

"Never mind," he said. "I was just going to say that we'll let Mr. Bond and Miss King enjoy each other for an evening. It's all part of the change in plan. As usual, Mr. Bond's attention will be focused on the wrong thing, and he won't go sticking his nose where it shouldn't belong later tonight," he went on. "He'll get his—and I'll get him—in due time. Come. We have a plane to catch."

They didn't say a word in the BMW on the way back to the villa. Gabor followed at a discreet distance. They eventually pulled in through the gate, parked, and walked to the front of the house. Anticipation was thick in the air. Bond opened the door for Elektra, and she swept through. She moved to the circular stairway and began to ascend. Bond lingered a moment in the open doorway. His eyes followed her, locked on her magnificent body.

Elektra paused halfway up the stairs. She looked down at him. She hesitated, but he waited for her to make the first move. He knew that she would.

Slowly, she held out her hand. Her mouth parted, silently beckoning him. Bond rushed up the stairs and joined her, their mouths meeting in a passionate kiss. She moaned and went limp in his arms, allowing him to take control. He picked her up and carried her into the bedroom.

The tension of the last few days had caught up with them. They pulled at each other's clothes as the sound of heavy breathing filled the air. She ran her hands through his hair and lightly scratched his cheek as she kissed him. He broke the zipper at the back of her dress. She gasped when she heard the ripping noise, but this only seemed to excite her more.

She pulled him to the bed and bit his lower lip as he kissed her. She arched her back as his hands slid over her sleek body. Her moans went from soft whimpers to throaty cries of passion.

They made love slowly, languorously. It was something that couldn't be rushed. The fire within them burned deeply, and together they coaxed it out of their bodies until sweat beaded on their skin.

After their first orgasms, they lay in each other's arms and breathed steadily. Her hand traced the contours of his torso, the fingers lingering on the bruised, left collarbone.

"I knew when I first saw you," she whispered. "I knew it would be like this."

"Shhhh," Bond said, kissing her neck.

Her hand dipped into an ice bucket beside the bed. She brought a sliver of ice up and down her chest, between her full breasts and across her swollen nipples. Elektra shuddered with pleasure as the cold penetrated the warm skin, sending bolts of delight throughout her body. It was a move Bond hadn't seen before. Then she rubbed the ice against Bond's sore shoulder.

"You poor thing," she murmured. "Looks painful . . ."

She kissed the purple flesh and licked the water running off the melting ice.

"Needs constant attention," Bond said, lapping the drips from the top of her right breast.

She slid her tongue back and forth along the groove

above the tendon. She had already proved that she could do things with her tongue that most men only dreamed about. This was only further evidence of her skills.

"Enough ice for one day," Bond said as he gently took the ice out of her hand and tossed it across the room.

The passion took over for a second time that night.

Later, after they were spent, Bond opened a bottle of vintage champagne and the pillow talk began again. As he caressed her naked back, tracing the curve of her spine, she asked him about his life. He revealed what he told most lovers, concentrating mostly on the particular trivialities of the world that interested him. They talked of food and drink, traveling, and about the thrill of sport. They shared a love for skiing and the rush of adrenaline it provided. They listed what they loved and hated about London. She spoke of music and art, and he expressed an admiration of Eastern philosophy. They discussed sex and what they each found desirable. She admitted that none of her former lovers had come near satisfying her the way Bond had.

She told him of her dreams and goals, and how she wanted to make her father's company a world player. "When I was a little girl," she said, "I played 'princess' a lot. My father spoiled me. He used to call me his 'little princess.' He would tell me that when I grew up, I really would be a princess. It sounds horrible, but I suppose I've always believed that. It inspired me to work at it, though. Even though he spoiled me, I never took it for granted. I miss him."

"I was under the impression that you and your father didn't get along," Bond said.

She laughed. "Who told you that? Davidov, I would imagine. That's only because he had the pleasure of seeing us when we *did* quarrel. I said my father was good at quarreling; well, I think I inherited that attractive trait from him. We could get into furious fights over business decisions, but it didn't mean we didn't love each other. I respect my father and he respected me. I earned my place in King Industries. I worked hard at university. And he knew I had what it took."

"My superior at MI6 thought very highly of him," Bond said.

"Dear M," Elektra said. "What a lady. She is very maternal toward me."

"Tell me about your mother," Bond said.

"I remember that she was kind, but quiet and shy. Introverted. She spoke very quietly, almost in a whisper. She came from a very cultured family that wasn't very smart in business, I'm afraid. My father, well, he saved their business, but he had to take it from them to do it. My mother died when I was six years old. It was one of those cancers that hit unexpectedly and spread rapidly. I don't remember a lot about it except that it was a very painful time in my life. To tell the truth, I don't remember too many happy times before then, either."

"Why is that?"

"My parents . . . they quarreled. A lot. It's practically the only thing I remember about their relationship. Come to think of it, I think they mostly quarreled about me. Sometimes I wonder why they got married. Oh, I'm sure they loved each other, but they were very different people. Two different cultures. Even so, my father was constantly at her side during the illness, and she died in the hospital, holding his hand."

"I'm sorry."

"I look back and I realize that I don't have too many memories of my mother. After all, I was young when she died. I remember a lullaby that she used to sing to me. It's one of the few pleasant memories I have of her."

She began to sing, slowly and softly, a haunting melody. Then she looked up at him and smiled. "The first words have no meaning. The rest is 'Calves entered the vegetable garden; gardener, drive away the calves, don't let them eat the cabbage . . . Sleep, my baby, sleep, sleep and grow up, drive away the calves, nenni, my little sweet baby, nenni.' I never really got to know my mother. I don't know why. She was afraid . . . of something. I don't know what. Of life, perhaps."

After a moment's reflection, she continued. "As I grew up, I was the exact opposite. I couldn't get enough out of life. I was my father's princess. He promised me the world and I guess I got it before I thought I would."

"You seem to be doing a fine job running the company."

"Thanks. You don't know how passionate I am about finishing the pipeline. It's something that will make history, I know it. I owe it to my father to finish it, certainly, but you know what? I owe it to my mother more. If it hadn't been for her family's oil company, and their land that my father developed early on . . . we wouldn't be here today. My mother's ancestors clung to their oil for years. It's a matter of honor."

She put into words what Bond found attractive about

her. It was the passion she embodied—whether it was for her work, for sport, her love for her parents, or for the fervent sex that she so thoroughly enjoyed.

As he rubbed the muscles in her shoulders, Bond focused on an unusual jewel in her earlobe. It was the ear he had seen bandaged in the kidnappers' Polaroid. The base of the diamond was wide, covering something on the skin.

Their eyes met. She knew what he was pondering. Tenderly, he reached out and touched the jewel. She didn't stop him.

"He used a pair of wire cutters on it," she said. "He said he was going to cut my whole ear off and send it to my father. I don't know why he didn't."

"Can you tell me about him?"

"His name was Renard. I've heard him called Renard the Fox. I learned that from your people after . . . after it was all over. He was . . . horrible. He shouted a lot. He made me . . . do things. He hit me. He snipped my earlobe with wire cutters. It was three weeks of hell. I'm afraid I'll never fully get over it."

Bond again thought of M's directive not to let her know that it was Renard who was trying to kill her. He could discern that most of the time Elektra was fine and in control. She was a bit reckless, perhaps, but she seemed to be on top of the business. Nevertheless, he had seen glimpses of a vulnerable, frightened girl who most assuredly still had nightmares about the terrible thing that had happened to her. Renard was probably the demon in her dreams, and it was best that she didn't know he was close to her once again.

"How did you survive?" he asked her.

She closed her eyes and spoke slowly, as if she could revisit the incident only in the far reaches of her mind. "I seduced a guard. Used my body. It gave me control. There was one guard who couldn't help himself. He had to have me. When the moment was right, I kicked him in his most vulnerable spot. I got a gun, and I just started shooting. I killed . . . three men. Renard wasn't there at the time or I would have killed him, too."

She trembled a moment. The memory had struck a nerve. She pulled closer to him, nuzzling her face in his chest and stifling a sob. Another chill went down her spine and she shuddered again.

Bond was affected by the story of her ordeal, but he said nothing.

"For someone so in love with life, I wanted to die," she said. "For months afterward, I was a vegetable. But then . . . something snapped. I realized that I had to pull myself out of the lower depths. I hate to say it, but I think my father's murder may have had something to do with shaking me back to the real world. Someone had to take charge." She paused a moment to take a sip of champagne. "But what about you? What do you do to survive?"

The truthful answer to that was that he never looked back. Bond didn't want to reveal too much of himself, though. Instead, he turned the question around and focused it on her.

"I take pleasure . . ." he said, "in great beauty."

For the third time that night their bodies came together. This time, they made it last an eternity.

8

Journey at Dawn

Bond left Elektra sleeping in her room a couple of hours before sunrise. He quietly made his way to his room, changed into dark clothes, grabbed a few items that might be of use, and crept outside. Two guards on patrol crossed in front of the building. Bond hid in an alcove until they were out of sight, then ran around to the side of the building. He leaped and caught a tree branch beside the fence, swung up and over, and dropped to the other side. He ran to the security annex, where Sasha Davidov kept his office.

The automatic lock pick from Q Branch came in handy on the heavy door. With a touch of a button, the device sent sound waves into the lock; there was a _click_ and the door opened. Bond stepped inside and shut the door, locking it behind him. Despite having two windows, the office was quite dark, so he held a penlight in his mouth while he searched through desk drawers and filing cabinets. None of it was of any interest—mostly papers, a few pistol magazines, office supplies . . .

He was about to examine a carryall sitting on the floor under the desk when a car's headlamps shone through the front of the little building. The entire room was bathed in light through the window, but Bond stepped to the side and hid in the shadows. He looked out and saw a Land Rover with the now familiar Russian Atomic Energy Department symbols on the side. Sasha Davidov got out of the driver's seat and looked around furtively. This was a man who didn't want to be seen, Bond thought. He also noticed that Davidov's hand was bandaged and that he was carrying a briefcase.

Davidov moved out of the line of sight. Bond had to move fast. Keys clattered against the lock, and in a moment the door opened.

Davidov stepped inside and turned on the lights. The office was empty, but a breeze was blowing in through an open window. Not suspecting a thing, the Russian slammed the window shut and locked it.

Outside, Bond quietly got up from the cool, dark ground beneath the window and hid behind the Land Rover. He peered into the now illuminated office window and watched as Davidov removed something from the briefcase and sat at his desk. The man took a tool from a drawer and intently worked on whatever object was in his hands.

Bond moved to the back of the vehicle and opened

the hatch. There was an envelope full of papers next to a tarpaulin that covered something bulky. Bond pulled it back and got a mild shock. It was a corpse, an older man, with a bullet hole in his head. A sudden flash of light from the security annex diverted Bond's attention from the truck. Looking at the window again, he saw that Davidov was holding a Polaroid camera at arm's length and taking a picture of himself.

Considering this, Bond turned again to the dead body in the Land Rover. The corpse was dressed in overalls with the Russian logo plastered on the sleeve. Bond noted that the shirt pocket was torn, probably where an ID card had been attached.

A torch beam swerved across the road. One of the patrolling guards was approaching. Bond jumped inside the Land Rover and quietly pulled the hatch down.

Davidov drove the Land Rover to an airfield hidden in the woods approximately eight miles away. He was nervous as hell. Renard had scared him badly, he admitted to himself. And poor Arkov . . . All he had done was to suggest that the mission be called off. He, Davidov, would have to be extra careful or he, too, would end up with a bullet in the head. And not a bullet like Renard's.

At least Arkov had been successful in obtaining the Antonov AN-12 Cub, a Russian military transport plane, which sat on the well-lit runway. Men in overalls surrounded the aircraft, some on top of scaffolding. They were busy plastering Russian Atomic Energy decals on the fuselage and tail. A searchlight swept the airfield, looking for anything that shouldn't be there.

Davidov drove to the small wooden shed that served as the airfield's office. He backed up to a debris skip next to the building and parked. He got out and peered through the stand of trees that separated the shed from the runway. The plane was almost ready. He had better get prepared.

His boots crunched on the tarmac as he moved around the Land Rover and opened the rear hatch. Now for the disgusting part . . .

He pushed aside the tarp and grabbed hold of the body.

"Up we go—" Davidov said.

The corpse's head turned and smiled. Davidov gasped.

James Bond swung a backhand at Davidov, but it was only a glancing blow. Davidov reeled backward and pulled a gun from his coat; Bond was faster. A single shot from 007's silenced Walther cut the air with a *pffft* and sent Davidov to the ground. Bond climbed out of the hatch, glanced through the trees at the plane, then crouched beside the dead Head of Security. Sure enough, the ID card of the corpse he had found was clipped to Davidov's jacket. Davidov's freshly taken Polaroid was crudely pasted on top of what was assuredly the dead man's face. His name was Arkov . . .

Bond pulled off the card and pocketed it, then scanned the area for a safe place to hide the body. The debris skip . . .

Bond leaned in to pick up the corpse when Davidov's cell phone on his belt rang. Bond froze. It rang a second time. If Davidov didn't answer . . .

Bond picked it up and spoke Russian. "Yes?"

A low voice at the other end said, "One—five—eight—nine—two. Copy?"

"Yes." Was it Renard?

"Out." The line went dead. Bond clipped the phone to his own belt, then heaved Davidov's body over his shoulder. A beam of light played along the trees between the runway and the Land Rover. Someone was coming!

Bond threw the corpse into the skip just as a large Russian man in overalls emerged from the woods. "Let's go!" he said. "It's getting late!"

When the man saw Bond's face and didn't see another man with him, he registered surprise. "What happened to Davidov?" he asked, ready to pull a gun. "I was told to expect him, too."

"He was up to his eyes in work," Bond said in Russian. "He told me to go on alone."

The man hesitated, then relaxed and shrugged. "Got your stuff? Let's go."

Bond moved to the Land Rover and looked in the back. What should he take? The carryall he had seen earlier in the office was there, along with the envelope and Davidov's briefcase.

"Well?" the man asked.

Bond grabbed the carryall and the envelope, which he thrust into his inside jacket pocket, and followed the man to the runway. The plane's engine had fired up and he could sense a feeling of urgency among the men.

"I'm Truhkin," the man said. "You must be Arkov."

Bond grunted affirmatively. The workers had finished with the plane. It now looked as if it belonged to the

Russian agency. The Russian pilot approached Bond anxiously.

"You're late!" he shouted. "You got a squawk?"

Bond's eyes narrowed in confusion.

"A squawk! The transponder codes! If we're not squawking the right code, they'll shoot us down!"

Bond hesitated, then said, "One—five—eight—nine—two?"

The pilot nodded, then looked him up and down. His brow creased when he saw Bond's formal-looking shoes. He glared at Bond in a way clearly meant to be intimidating. "And the rest? Did you bring the grease?"

Bond didn't have a clue what the man was talking about. The pilot stared, expectantly. With no choice but to wing it, Bond opened the carryall. He reached inside and, to his relief, found a box of Adidas trainers.

The pilot beamed when Bond revealed them. "Excellent!"

The Antonov Cub flew at 482 miles per hour toward the rising sun, then turned north, crossing the Caspian Sea into west-central Asia. The pilot, in his overalls and new Adidas, whistled happily in the cockpit.

Bond sat in the rear between heavily secured cargo pallets. Everything was marked in Russian characters, which Bond easily translated as warnings: DANGER—RADIOACTIVE. There was an empty berth on one side of the aircraft, large enough for an automobile. Truhkin had expressly forbidden him to place anything there.

Whatever Renard was planning, Bond had stumbled onto it. He thought about Elektra, and wondered if she would be worried about him. There had been few occasions during his career in which Bond felt nervous about going undercover. This was definitely one of them. He just hoped that he could improvise his role well enough to find out what this was all about and then get out alive.

Truhkin appeared, his tall frame crouched over in the fuselage. He tossed a windbreaker bearing the Russian logo at Bond.

"Get ready," he said. "Ten minutes and we'll be in Kazakhstan. And make sure you wear the ID."

Bond nodded as the Russian went back to his seat up front. Bond got up and went into the lavatory. He shut the door, then removed his wallet. He got Arkov's ID out of his pocket and placed it on the counter. Next, he bent over and pried open the heel of his SIS field shoe. Inside were useful items such as a small pair of scissors, tape, a screwdriver . . . Bond took the scissors and tape and set to work.

He took out his "Universal Exports" ID card and carefully cut out his picture. He replaced the card in his wallet and put it back in his pocket. Using the edge of the scissors, he scraped Davidov's new photo from the ID, revealing the face of the corpse he had found in the Land Rover. Bond affixed his own photo to the ID card with the tape and attached it to his shirt pocket. *Well,* he thought. *Let's hope that no one knows the real Dr. Arkov by sight wherever the plane is headed.*

The plane entered Kazakhstan airspace as Bond sat back down in the fuselage. A newly independent country, Kazakhstan was another former Soviet-controlled state that was struggling to keep on its feet. It seemed that all of the countries in the Commonwealth of Independent States had the same problems—rampant crime in the face of a new capitalism, ethnic disputes, and regular economic and political upheaval. Most of what Bond knew about Kazakhstan concerned the Russian-operated space launch facility, the Baikonur Cosmodrome, in the center of the country. He also knew, though, that the country was rich in coal, oil, and gas. He had to wait and see exactly what connection the Russian nuclear agency had with Renard, Davidov, and for that matter, King Industries.

The Cub landed at dawn in the western part of the country, in a place of desolation, salt basins, and deserts. It was a vast region of strange rock formations and rough terrain. The sun's heat was already elevating to a desert-like temperature.

Bond followed Truhkin to another Land Rover, again marked with the Russian Atomic Energy Department logo.

"I'll drive," Truhkin said. "First time in Kazakhstan?"

"Yes," Bond said.

"Lovely place," Truhkin said sarcastically as they drove away from the makeshift airfield and onto a dirt road. They went through a rock valley that was decidedly alien in appearance, then eventually came upon a huge mesa with a huddle of low buildings beneath it. As they got closer, Bond could see trucks, Kazakhstani Army personnel carriers, soldiers, and other men in overalls at work.

An explosion off to one side startled them both. A

cloud of dust rose from a detonation site five hundred yards away.

When he saw the trucks marked IDA, Bond knew where they were. It was a Russian nuclear testing facility, most likely owned by the Russian Atomic Energy Department. The IDA, or International Decommissioning Authority, was a United Nations–sponsored organization that was responsible for managing the decommissioning of nuclear reactors and other radioactive facilities used for research and development in a safe and environmentally sensitive manner.

They got out of the Land Rover and approached the main building, the entrance of which was covered by a protective, inflated "bubble." Bond could make out someone inside the bubble wearing a radiation-proof suit and tinkering with objects and tools.

A Russian army colonel was standing at the entrance to the bubble. When he saw Bond's ID card, he smiled, obviously impressed.

"Welcome to Kazakhstan, Dr. Arkov!" he said in Russian. "I am Colonel Akakievich. I'm a great admirer of your research. It's not often we see someone of your stature here."

Bond replied, "I go where the work takes me."

The colonel hesitated a moment. "You *do* have the transport documents . . . ?"

Bond patted his jacket and found the envelope he had fortuitously placed there earlier. He handed it over, hoping for the best.

Colonel Akakievich gave the papers a once-over and nodded toward the bubble. "Good. They're waiting for you below. It should be ready. Check with the IDA physicist."

The figure in the white radiation-proof suit emerged from the bubble. The helmet came off, revealing a most attractive young woman with long, light brown hair. She was sweating profusely and paused to take a cloth from a rack and wipe her forehead with it. Then she undid the suit and stepped out of it. She was wearing very short cutoffs, a khaki sports bra, heavy-duty boots, and a hunting knife. Bond guessed that she was an American.

She had an extraordinary figure. Her breasts bulged beneath the bra, and her legs were tanned, sleek, and shapely. Bond noticed that every man in the vicinity stopped what he was doing to gawk at her.

The girl grabbed a bottle of water and guzzled, letting the liquid dribble down her chin and onto her top. Next, she poured the bottle over her shoulders until she was soaking. The clothes clung to her tight body, and her hardened nipples could be seen plainly through the bra. Either she was an exhibitionist, Bond thought, or she just didn't give a damn.

Bond's eyes met the colonel's. Akakievich nodded bitterly, then spat on the floor. He said, in English, so that she could hear, "Not interested in men. Take my word for it. We decommissioned four test sites this year . . . and not even a glimmer."

Bond offered a disappointed "tut-tut" as the colonel walked away.

The girl stepped up to Bond, wiping her rather wide mouth. She had amazing green eyes and sparkling white teeth. Bond guessed that she was probably in her mid-twenties. He couldn't help but notice the IDA tag on her belt and the incongruous peace-sign tattoo just above her hip.

"Are you here for a reason?" she asked. She gestured to the colonel. "Or are you just hoping for a 'glimmer'?"

Bond attempted a light Russian accent, but spoke English. "It would appear the nuclear weapons are not the only thing around here that need defusing."

The girl frowned. "Nice try. And you are?"

"Mikhail Arkov," he said. "Russian Atomic Energy Department. And you are—Miss—"

"Doctor. Jones. Christmas Jones," she said. "And don't make any jokes. I've heard them all."

"I don't know any doctor jokes," he said.

She gave him a dirty look. "Give me the papers. Where's the shipment going?"

"The nuclear facility at Penza Nineteen," Bond said. That much he had gleaned from a cursory scan. He handed them to her. "I apologize if my countrymen give you a hard time. I know they're not all happy to see the International Decommissioning Authority here."

Dr. Jones handed the papers back. "Now, if you'll excuse me, I've got a leaking titanium trigger to look after. I just got through removing a sphere of cobalt—blue plutonium from a corroding warhead. I lead a very exciting existence."

Bond smiled and nodded, but quite obviously didn't know where he was supposed to go.

She gestured to the building. "Take the elevator down the hole. Your friends are already down there."

"Don't I need some kind of . . . protection?" Bond asked.

She looked askance, as if Dr. Arkov should know better. "Not unless there's a leaking titanium trigger I don't know about. Down there are fission bombs. Weapons-grade plutonium. Low radiation risk. It's not hot. Up here we've got hydrogen bombs—that *your* lab built—leaking tritium—which I've spent the last six months trying to clean up. So if you need any protection at all, it's from me."

"Right," Bond said sheepishly. "And here I thought we'd abandoned the doctrine of mutually assured destruction. Thanks."

The charm wasn't working. She pointed to the lift again. "That way. They're waiting."

He walked toward the elevator, passing a board filled with radioactivity badges.

"Doctor?" she called.

Bond turned back to her.

"Aren't you forgetting something?"

He realized that he'd made a mistake. It was so basic that he could tell she was suspicious now. He took one of the badges from the board.

"Right. Of course. Thank you," he said. "It was a long flight."

He continued toward the lift, when she called after him, in Russian, "Your English is very good for a Russian."

Bond replied, in Russian, "I studied at Oxford."

Christmas watched him disappear into the building and once again wiped the sweat from her brow. *Hmm,* she thought. *This* one was different! Dark and handsome, for a change, if a little screwy. Something wasn't right, though . . .

She took another drink of water, then went about her business.

The lift took Bond down into the ground past three levels. When the doors opened, he found himself completely alone and facing a long, dark, circular corridor. It was dead quiet.

He walked forward until he could hear the sound of machinery and an ominous humming. There was a larger, illuminated room up ahead.

It was a spherical test chamber, surrounded by blast openings designed to channel the fury of a nuclear test to measuring equipment. In the very center of the chamber was a pit. He was standing in one of several similar tunnels that radiated from the chamber. Bond entered the eerie place, slowly stepped to the middle, and looked over into the hole. Four men were working on a device on top of a cart. The head had been removed and much of its guts were exposed. Nevertheless, Bond knew that it was an atomic bomb.

Renard's voice came from behind. "Beautiful, isn't it?"

9

Fire in the Hole

At the sound of Renard's voice, Bond whipped out the Walther. The whine of a lift began and Bond saw Renard, dressed in Russian army fatigues, lowering himself on a platform. Bond stole through the shadows to meet the terrorist, keeping his head down as Renard descended. As Renard stepped off the lift, Bond came face-to-face with him and smiled. The gun was pointing at Renard's chest.

"Mr. Bond," Renard said, obviously surprised.

"Expecting Davidov perhaps?" Bond asked. "He caught a bullet instead of the plane." He yanked Renard away from the lift and shoved him against a wall, out of sight. "Keep your mouth shut. Don't move."

Renard all but laughed. "You can't kill me, Mr. Bond," he said. "I'm already dead."

"Not dead enough for me."

Finally confronting the man who was responsible for murdering Sir Robert King, 0012, and countless others . . . as well as raping and kidnapping Elektra King . . . Bond had to control himself to keep from blowing Renard's brains out then and there. It would have been a pleasure. Unfortunately, he needed a bit more time, during which the terrorist might reveal a little of the scheme he had concocted. Such people always did.

Renard had shrugged away his surprise and now appeared to be fully confident. He looked at Bond with a twinkle in his good eye. The other one stared straight ahead, unblinking, cold and lifeless. A smile played on half of Renard's face, but the other corner of his mouth turned down in a grimace. The shiny red lump at his temple only added to the man's bizarre appearance.

"You could show a little gratitude. I *did* spare your life in the banker's office." Renard was beginning to enjoy himself. "Oh! But that's right! I couldn't kill you. You were working for *me*! I needed you to deliver the money. To kill King. Thank you for that. Well done. And now you've brought me the plane. It seems that I can always count on MI6."

Bond ignored the taunt. "What's your plan with that bomb?"

Renard seemed totally fearless. "You first. Or could it be you don't have a plan?"

Unfortunately, he had spoken an uncomfortable truth. Bond needed to buy time in order to work out what to do.

"That bomb won't leave this room," he said.

"Neither will you," Renard said, chuckling.

Bond risked a glance at the pit to see what the workers were doing with the bomb.

"How sad," Renard continued. "To be threatened by a man who can't grasp what he's caught up in. You haven't a clue, have you?"

"Revenge isn't hard to fathom from a man who believes in nothing."

Renard laughed. "And what do you believe in? Preservation of capital? You're nothing but a dim-witted bouncer at a fancy English club run by your betters. Too busy chasing the members' daughters to do your job. Shoot me. I welcome it. The men down there will hear the shot. They will kill you and get away with the bomb."

"The firefight will bring down half those troops from the surface."

"Perhaps. But when a certain phone call isn't received in twenty minutes . . ." He said into Bond's face, "Go ahead. Pull the trigger, and you'll kill Elektra."

"You're bluffing."

"Beautiful, isn't she?" Renard said. "I think you've fallen for her. I can see it on your face. Well, my friend, you should have had her before. When she was innocent. Before she was such a whore in bed."

Bond's eyes flared in fury. He shoved Renard against the wall again and pressed the gun into his temple.

"How does it feel?" Renard continued, knowing he had hit a nerve. "To know I broke her in for you?"

Furious, Bond struck Renard across the temple with the pistol. The terrorist dropped to his knees. He touched his head, then looked curiously at the blood on his fingers. He felt no pain at all.

Bond screwed on the silencer. "I usually hate killing an unarmed man. Cold-blooded murder is filthy business. But in your case, I feel nothing. Just like you." He held the gun down, aiming at Renard's head.

"A man tires of being executed," Renard said. "But then again, there is no point in living if you can't . . . feel alive."

Bond was about to squeeze the trigger when the sound of running footsteps interrupted him.

"Drop the gun," Colonel Akakievich commanded. Bond froze. He turned to see the colonel with two armed soldiers and Dr. Christmas Jones.

"Keep away, Colonel," Bond said. The soldiers trained their guns on Bond.

"He's an impostor," Christmas said. She held up a printout. "Dr. Arkov is sixty-three years old."

"Here's your impostor," Bond said, indicating Renard. "Along with the men on the plane outside. They're stealing your bomb, Colonel."

Christmas, surprised by the change in Bond's accent, listened, but Akakievich cocked his rifle.

"I said drop it," the colonel ordered.

He clearly meant it. Bond delayed another second . . . but had no choice. He pulled the magazine from his gun and tossed it down. At that moment, a whirring sound filled the room as machinery in the pit came to life. The cone-shaped bomb, enclosed in a carrying cage, rose into view as Renard's men quickly manipulated a robot arm to place the extremely heavy device on a wheeled cart. Then they attached the cage to an overhead track with chains so that it could be pushed through the tunnel more easily.

"Well done," Renard said to Christmas. "He would have killed us all." Then, to Akakievich: "I suppose you were the one who allowed him down?"

The colonel looked suitably embarrassed.

So, Bond thought, Renard and the Russian colonel were in this together. But what about the girl? Was she a part of their cabal? From the confused look on her face, Bond guessed not. She was being used, too. The doctor was staring at him now, wondering if she had just made a huge mistake.

Bond watched as one of the men referred to a Russian manual just like the one he had seen in M's office and then removed a thin metal rectangular object from inside the bomb. It was the size of a credit card. The man slipped it into his shirt pocket.

"Take him away," Renard said to the colonel. "I don't want him here when we move the bomb." He then stepped close to Bond and whispered, "You had me. But I knew you couldn't shoulder the responsibility . . ."

With that, Renard jammed his hand into Bond's bad collarbone, squeezing hard. Pain jolted through Bond as he dropped to his knees in agony. He held his shoulder and grimaced, but his mind raced. How did Renard know to hurt him there?

Renard then approached Christmas, who was petrified with fear. "I'm sorry, my dear, but you have to join our other guest," he said. "It's too bad you had to witness all of this." He turned to his men. "Now, without any further interruptions, let's get on with it!"

The men maneuvered the bomb toward the curving passageway.

"Nyet," Colonel Akakievich said. "The bomb doesn't move until I am satisfied. I want my payment. You owe me. All of you, to the surface, now."

Renard stopped and turned. "You're right, Colonel." He nodded to two of his men. One quietly slipped away down the tunnel. The other innocently opened a container filled with frozen-food packs. He released a false lining in the lid to reveal several machine guns.

"We'll all go up," Renard said. "I admire your devotion to the cause."

One of the colonel's men gestured with his gun for Bond to get up. Knowing it was now or never, Bond pushed him away, yanked the pistol from his hand, grabbed Christmas, and leaped down into the bomb pit just as Renard's men opened fire. Colonel Akakievich and two soldiers were perforated. The bullets ricocheted around the chamber and ceased. One of the men carefully approached the pit, but he was forced back by a grazing shot from Bond's gun.

"Forget them," Renard said. He spoke into his radio. "Shut them in."

A man at the other end of the radio, next to the lift, turned a switch that activated two red buttons and two green ones. He punched one green button and heavy iris-shaped steel doors sealed all the tunnels but the one leading to the lift. Renard and his three men started to push the bomb cart into this tunnel. It was slow, hard work. After a few minutes, Renard became impatient and ran ahead. He began to pull the bomb along on the overhead tracks, leaving the cart behind. His henchmen were amazed; he seemed to have the strength of three men.

Bond and Christmas heard the hum of the doors closing.

"They're sealing us in!" Christmas said.

"We'll find a way out. Quickly!"

"Who *are* you?" she asked.

Bond looked around the pit, forming a plan. "I work for the British government."

Acting quickly, he pointed his wristwatch toward the catwalk above. He pressed a button and the tiny grappling hook shot out with Q's filament wire. The hook caught onto a metal beam and stuck. Bond gave the line a tug to make sure it was secure, then rappelled up the side of the pit and into the test chamber. He dived through the iris of the doors just as they slammed shut behind him. The nearest man swung his machine gun around, but Bond got off a shot first. The man fell and Bond ran to him. He was the one who had extracted the rectangular object from the bomb. Bond reached into his shirt, retrieved it, and put it into his own pocket.

Bond then ran behind the abandoned cart and fired a couple of shots down the tunnel at Renard. Return fire ripped up the wall next to him. He ducked behind the cart until the barrage subsided. As he lay on his back, he got an idea. He aimed the pistol at the overhead work lights and shot them all out. His end of the tunnel was plunged into darkness; Renard and his men now had no visible target.

Meanwhile, in the pit, Christmas Jones managed to climb up the side to the closed iris door. She found a panel next to it and pried it open, revealing a mess of wiring. She started to work with the only tools she had . . . her fingers.

No longer a sitting duck, Bond inched out from behind the cart and fired toward the dimly lit figures in the tunnel.

A bullet grazed Renard's arm. He clasped the wound, again noting the blood and the strange lack of sensation. One of his two remaining men sprayed the dark end of the corridor with gunfire. Renard and the other man continued to pull the bomb along the track. Shots from the opposite end of the tunnel whizzed past them.

"Arrggh!" Renard's helper gasped. One of Bond's rounds had hit him in the back. Moaning, he hung on to the bomb, impeding its progress. Renard tugged at it.

"Let go!" he shouted at the man. The wounded thug clung to the device, pleading for help. Renard pulled his gun and aimed it at the man's head.

"Here, this should help," he said, squeezing the trigger.

Two minutes later, Renard and his one remaining companion managed to clear a second set of blast doors at the midway point. He shouted into his radio, "Close the middle doors!"

Bond heard the command. Using all of his strength, he pushed the abandoned cart forward, using it as cover. Suddenly the doors started closing. Bond realized that he wasn't going to make it; with a superhuman effort he shoved the cart ahead of him so that it was caught in the closing doors, holding them back for a heartbeat—just long enough for him to take a diving leap through before the doors crushed the cart and sealed shut.

As soon as Bond hit the ground on the other side of the doors, he was fired upon. He rolled to the side for cover and shot out a few more lights above him. He then paused to reload.

Inside the pit, Christmas connected two colored wires. The blast doors began to open. She glanced out and saw that the midsection doors were still shut. She returned to the control panel and continued working.

Diving and shooting, Bond managed to progress three-quarters of the way up the tunnel. The man at the door controls fired back, attempting to pin Bond down.

Renard and his man were finally successful in getting the bomb past a pile of oil drums and wrestling it into the lift.

"Let's go!" Renard shouted to the man at the controls. The thug raked the switches with gunfire, blowing them out, then raced for the lift. Unfortunately, the clear Lexsan bulletproofed doors closed on his face before he could get inside. Stunned, he turned to see Bond rushing toward him. The Walther PPK spat fire and the man dropped to the floor.

Through the doors, Bond could see Renard and his man standing next to the bomb. Bond fired at Renard, but the bullets bounced off the Lexsan. The cab began to rise.

Renard smiled and shouted, "No hard feelings, Mr. Bond! We're even. Soon you'll feel nothing at all!" He pointed down.

The cab disappeared up the shaft, and in its place was another bomb, rising into view. It wasn't an atomic bomb, but it looked extremely formidable. The LED was ticking off the seconds: 10 ... 9 ... 8 ... Horrified, Bond turned to see that the door switch panel was shredded. He was trapped. Then he heard the familiar hum of the iris doors opening behind him. Dr. Jones!

Looking up, Bond noticed the pulley hook that was used to move Renard's bomb along the overhead track. He made a running jump, grabbed it, and slid on the track toward the iris door.

Behind him, the bomb went off, igniting the oil drums. The fireball expanded, almost overtaking Bond on the pulley. Miraculously, the iris opened and Bond shot through at the right second. He saw that the next door was also open, and Christmas was standing just beyond.

"Seal the door! Close it!" Bond shouted.

Christmas's eyes widened at the sight of Bond hurtling toward her with a massive fireball in pursuit. She turned to the control panel and sparked the wires. The iris began to close just as Bond, followed by two flying oil barrels, sailed through. The barrels clattered down into the pit and burst into flame. As the fire licked the sides, Bond frantically searched for a way out and saw the arm of the robot lifter stretching toward an old shaft at the top of the ceiling. An abandoned lift? He took the chance that it might still be operational.

"Up! Go!" he shouted. He gave Christmas a boost. She grabbed the arm and crawled up and through some girders. Bond jumped up behind her and they emerged onto a catwalk just as the flames spread across the floor of the test center.

"No time to stop," Bond said, pulling her forward.

"Those barrels down there will blow." They ran to the end of the walkway, where they indeed found an old hydraulic-powered lift.

"I'm sure this old thing won't work," she said, her voice shaking.

"We'll never know unless we try!"

They got inside and Bond pushed the up button. The lift rumbled and then started to rise slowly. At that rate, they would suffocate. Bond peered over the side at the hydraulics.

"Hang on," he said.

"Okay," Christmas said. "So you're a British spy. Do you have a name?"

Bond aimed his gun at the hissing hydraulics. He gave her a look out the corner of his eye.

"The name is Bond . . ."

He fired the Walther. The hydraulic system blew out and the lift shot up through the shaft at breakneck speed, just as the entire pit exploded beneath them. Fire blew up the shaft, kissing the bottom of the cab. Bond lunged, covering Christmas. After a few moments, the smoke cleared.

". . . James Bond," he finished.

Outside the facility, Renard, Truhkin, and their last man pushed the bomb into the back of the Land Rover. They got in and drove quickly to the runway.

The lift stopped at the top of the shaft, but the doors refused to open. Christmas was coughing, blinded from the smoke. Soon there wouldn't be any oxygen left at all. Bond shone his illuminated wristwatch at the top of the cab and could make out a sealed duct cover.

"Hold your ears!" he shouted. He let off a few rounds at the edges of the cover. The noise reverberated deafeningly, but there were now thin beams of sunlight pouring into the cab.

"Can you give me a leg up?" he asked her. She nodded and clasped her hands together. Bond stepped into them, lifted himself, and pushed against the duct cover. He strained until Christmas cried, "I can't hold you much longer!"

Then the cover gave way, loosened by the bullet holes. Bond pulled himself up and out, then helped Christmas to do the same. They were standing in a cloud of dust some fifty feet from the main building. The heat of the sun had increased considerably.

Bond could make out people running about, panicked. Dead soldiers were on the ground. Then he heard the sound of jet engines.

"Come on!" he shouted, pulling her toward the runway, but they were too late. Renard's plane roared past them and lifted off. Bond followed it helplessly for a few steps, then gave up.

She caught up with him and said, "Hey, I'm sorry I blew the whistle on you. I had no clue what they were up to. I thought they were with the Russian Atomic Energy Department."

"Do you have any idea where they're going?"

"No, but they won't get far," Christmas said. "Every warhead has a GPS locator card. We can track the signal."

Bond took the object he had taken from the dead man and showed it to her. "You mean one of these?"

Her jaw dropped. "Damn," she said.

10

The Approaching Storm

B ill Tanner rushed into the Briefing Room at Castle Thane M16 headquarters shortly after M had arrived for the morning's work.

"I have something," he said. "It may not mean anything, but we should look into it."

M was standing with Robinson and other analysts, examining printouts from Interpol. Apparently, the terrorist known as Renard had been sighted in at least six different countries on the same day, and they had to sort out which reports were reliable, if any. M looked up and said, "Well?"

"We've been monitoring Russian military frequencies, of course. The Russian army has reported that one of their transport planes was stolen from an airfield in Omsk two days ago."

"So?"

"There's more. The Russian Atomic Energy Department is searching for some missing Parahawks and a nuclear physicist who's gone astray. A fellow named Arkov."

"What would any of that have to do with Renard?" M asked impatiently.

Tanner held up Sir Robert King's report. "Russian Atomic Energy Department," he said. "Dr. Arkov was supposed to be on assignment decommissioning a testing facility in Kazakhstan. Intelligence reports that the site was destroyed this morning and a Russian transport plane matching the description of the one that was stolen was seen leaving the area. The worst part is that they believe a bomb is missing."

"A bomb?"

"Plutonium-core warhead. The Russian army has put out an all-points arrest warrant for Colonel Akakievich, the officer who was in charge of the testing facility. Apparently he's gone missing, too, and they believe he may be involved. It's a long shot, but it just sounds like something Renard could be a part of."

M was perturbed that she hadn't put two and two together herself. "Right." She turned to Robinson. "Is there any way we can track that plane?"

Robinson almost laughed and pointed to the map. "It could be anywhere in this circle. Iran, Iraq, Pakistan, Syria, Afghanistan . . ."

"Marvelous," she said.

Moneypenny entered the room and got everyone's attention by announcing, "Elektra King is calling for M from Baku."

M was surprised. She went for the telephone, but Moneypenny said, "It's a video line."

"Put her on the wide screen."

Moneypenny made the connection, and Elektra's face materialized on the large wall monitor. She looked haggard and red-eyed.

"Hello," she said. "I'm sorry. I would never call you except . . . your man Bond has disappeared. He . . . he left my villa, sometime in the middle of the night."

M looked sideways at Tanner.

"He's been gone all day and hasn't returned. I thought you should know. There's already been one attempt on my life. And . . . my head of security has been found near a local airstrip, murdered . . ."

M leaned on the console in front of her. "I'll send someone else out right away."

Elektra furrowed her brow. "Could . . . could *you* come?"

M didn't expect that. The request so flustered her that at first she didn't know what to say. Then she studied the face of the girl who was like a daughter to her. Elektra King looked about as lost as she ever had.

"I just can't help thinking . . . that I'm next," Elektra said.

M stared at the girl on the screen, her whole sordid history written in her pleading eyes. M turned away from the screen and said to Tanner, "Get me out there."

Tanner started to protest. "Ma'am, I don't think—"

"Just do it!" She turned back to Elektra. "I'll be there as soon as possible. Don't leave your villa."

Elektra nodded, holding back tears of relief. "Thank you."

The connection was terminated.

"Where the devil is Double-O Seven?" M demanded.

"I'll try to find him," Robinson said, jumping to his station.

"M—" Tanner began, but M cut him short.

"I know what you're going to say, Chief of Staff, and I don't want to hear it," she said. "I'll take my bodyguard and Robinson. Miss Moneypenny, please make the necessary arrangements for immediate departure. I'd like to get to Baku before tomorrow. Tanner, you'll be in charge while I'm gone. See if you can track down that transport plane. And if you find Double-O Seven, you tell him that I'll speak to him *in person*."

Dark, black-and-blue storm clouds gathered off the coast of the choppy Caspian Sea. The wind howled and rattled the rafters of the King villa, creating an unsettling mood in what was already a rather dreary atmosphere.

Elektra sat alone in her father's study. As she worked by the halo of light from a single desk lamp, the room grew darker as the storm approached. She looked up from the latest geological reports from Turkey to relieve the strain on her eyes. A portrait of her father stared at her from the wall beside the desk. She felt a chill as the gale screeched outside. A window blew open, sending papers flying. Elektra got up, crossed the room, shut and locked the window. She stood there a moment, looking at the dark sky and the violent sea.

Inexplicably, Elektra thought of her mother. It happened, sometimes, especially when she was in this part of the world. Every so often, when these flashes of memory occurred, she could faintly hear the old lullaby her mother sang when Elektra was a little girl.

The sad, haunting tune reminded her of a cold, unfriendly past. A more superstitious person might have believed that a ghost was singing the song, but Elektra knew better.

At times, though, Elektra swore that she could still hear her mother's sobs as she lay dying in bed . . .

A loud thud from the library next door interrupted her reverie. She listened intently, but there was nothing else.

"Gabor?" she called.

She hesitated, then went to the study door and opened it. It whined on its hinges. She stepped into the large library, but it was pitch-dark and deathly quiet. Pale light from three French windows that led to a balcony barely illuminated the room. Elektra walked a few paces toward a lamp, but the door slammed shut behind her. She whirled around to see Gabor, propped up behind the door, staring, eyes wide. He fell to the floor like a rag doll. A dark figure stood in his place.

"Who's there?" she demanded.

The man stepped forward until the dim glow from the outside shone on his face. It was James Bond.

"James!" she cried. She couldn't hide the shock and hesitation in her voice.

"You sound surprised," he said.

She moved to Gabor, who was stirring and beginning to groan from the blow to the back of his head.

"What's wrong with you? Are you crazy?" she asked Bond.

"A little," Bond said. "Does it matter? After all, 'there's no point in living if you can't feel alive.' Isn't that right, Elektra? Isn't that your motto?"

"What the hell are you talking about?"

"Or did you steal it from your old friend Renard?"

Elektra wasn't sure she heard him right. "What?"

"He and I had a chat. He knew all about us, he knew about my shoulder, he knew exactly where I'd been hurt . . ." Bond said.

Elektra stood and began to tremble. "Are you saying . . . *Renard* is the man who's trying to kill me? He's *alive*?"

"You can drop the act, Elektra, it's over."

"I don't know what you're talking about!"

"I think you do." He walked toward her. His voice was laced with menace. "At M16 we call it Stockholm syndrome. It's common in kidnappings. A young impressionable victim. Sheltered, sexually inexperienced. A powerful kidnapper skilled in torture, in manipulation. Something snaps in the victim's mind. The captive falls in love with her captor."

At the word "love," Elektra exploded. She slapped Bond across the face.

"How dare you!" she spat. "How dare you! That animal? That monster? He disgusts me! *You* disgust me! So he knew where to hurt you, is that it? You had a

144

sling on your arm at the funeral! I didn't have to sleep with you to find that out."

"He used your exact words."

"What else have you *learned* while you left me all alone?"

"Your friend Davidov was in league with him."

"He's dead, as you no doubt know. You probably killed him." She shook her head. "Do you *really* believe that I would . . . with *Renard*?"

Bond let her continue to vent her anger. "You *knew*," she said. "You knew all the time that he was out there, that he was coming for me, and you lied. Wait a minute . . . I see it very clearly now. It's just like before. You *used* me. You and M16 used me as bait, although a more accurate term might be *meat*. Just like when I was kidnapped. M16 sent its little soldier to *protect* me when in fact you were hoping Renard would get close enough for you to catch him. You even made love to me—what, to pass the time as you waited for him to strike?"

He had no answer to that. He couldn't deny it.

Bond clenched his jaw. What if he was wrong? Could she be telling the truth? He had become suspicious during the long trip in Christmas's car from Kazakhstan back to Baku. Along the way, something about his encounter with Renard bothered him. He replayed the events over and over in his head. It was something Renard had said . . .

When he made the connection, Bond felt as if someone had just punched him in the stomach. The wave of dread that passed over him almost made him physically ill. Christmas had looked at him and asked, "What's the matter? You feel all right?" Bond had nodded and replied, "I'm just beginning to see this thing more clearly, that's all." For the remainder of the trip, he worked on purging his affection for Elektra King. He was certain that she was somehow connected with Renard's plans. He hardened his heart and put up the familiar stone-cold wall. It was painful, but it was not anything he hadn't done before.

Now Bond looked at Elektra and questioned his assumption. If she was truly in league with Renard, then she was a terrific actress. She was very convincing. She was right about his shoulder—Renard could have learned about that in other ways. Could those words have been a coincidence as well? *There's no point in living if you can't feel alive.*

Bond rarely believed in coincidences.

The phone on the library desk rang, cutting through the tension. She stared at him as it rang a second time . . . then a third. Finally, she picked it up.

"Yes?"

She listened for a moment. "I'm on my way." She hung up the phone and looked at Bond with daggers in her eyes. "He's struck again. The pipeline construction site. Five men are dead."

She turned to leave, but he moved after her. "I'm coming with you," he said.

"Do what you want. I need to call M back and tell her not to come here; she should meet me there."

"What?"

"Oh, didn't I say? I've already spoken to M once. She's coming to take charge."

That stopped Bond in his tracks. Elektra left the room, leaving him with Gabor, who was just managing to sit up. Bond sighed then helped the bodyguard to his feet.

M had flown from London to Istanbul, then used a Eurocopter EC 135 owned by the British military to take her to the pipeline control center. She arrived early the next morning, not long after Bond himself had returned from Baku with Christmas Jones. As the helicopter landed, M looked out of the window at the site, her face set hard.

It was clearly a disaster area. Five body bags had been laid out on the ground outside the industrial plant. Three buildings were demolished and the pipeline was damaged in four sections. Scientific, military, and police vehicles surrounded the place. Soldiers, policemen, and King Industries workers were sweeping the area. Interestingly, Renard's stolen transport plane was still standing on the airstrip.

Bond stood at the entrance of the building near Christmas, who was participating in the reconnaissance. He didn't like the look on M's face as she strode toward him with Robinson and her bodyguard in tow.

"Nice of you to join us, Double-O Seven," she said.

Bond ignored the quip and explained, "We still don't know if they did anything with the bomb here. There's a scientist from the International Decommissioning Agency over there—Dr. Jones. She's checking to see if she can find anything."

They stepped out of the bright sunlight and into the control center. The place was a shambles. Emergency illumination was in use until electricity could be restored. Technicians were busy tinkering with equipment that wasn't working. Elektra King was huddled with a couple of policemen. She nodded an acknowledgment to M. She had pointedly ignored Bond since their encounter in the library in Baku.

"Double-O Seven, I'd like a word," M said, pulling him aside. She threw a look to Robinson and the bodyguard, indicating that she wanted some privacy.

"I want an update," she said tersely. "Where do we stand?"

"Renard bribed people at the Russian Atomic Energy Department and in the Russian army. He got a transport plane and a bomb. I still don't know what he plans to do with it. Apparently, though, they landed here last night. Renard and his men killed several workmen, the security guards . . . Then they started to destroy things, as you can see. His motive is unclear. They left the stolen plane on the airstrip, and it's completely empty. It appears to me that he still has that bomb."

Bond took the locator card out of his pocket and handed it to her. "One of Renard's men removed this locator card from the bomb. So we can't track it."

She looked at it, turning it over.

"M . . ." He hesitated.

"What?"

"With all due respect," Bond said, "I don't think you should be here."

A flash of anger crossed M's face. "Need I remind you that you're the reason I'm here, Double-O Seven? You disobeyed a direct order, and left that girl alone."

"If I hadn't left her alone, we wouldn't know that Renard is in possession of a bomb. And perhaps that 'girl' isn't as innocent as you think."

"What are you saying?"

Bond brought his voice down further, stealing a glance at Elektra. "Suppose the inside man—the one who switched King's lapel pin—turned out to be an inside woman?"

M blinked, incredulous. "First she kills her father—then attacks her own pipeline. Why? To what end?"

"I don't know," Bond admitted. "Yet." His theory sounded even more absurd with M listening.

"Then let's deal with what we *do* know. We've got a dying terrorist with a nuclear bomb in his pocket. We don't know his plan, or where he's taken the weapon."

"Yes. But if it's revenge—to finish what he started in London—he's got *you* right where he wants you."

The lights suddenly powered up as the workers succeeded in restoring electricity. The monitors that lined the room flashed on, and a huge satellite map of the pipeline appeared on a wall-sized screen. The technicians scrambled to their posts to inspect the machinery's usability.

"M . . ." Elektra called. She was studying the pipeline map.

"We'll talk about this later, Double-O Seven," M said, then moved toward Elektra.

"Look at this," Elektra said, pointing to a flashing red light. "That's not right. It shouldn't be there."

Robinson asked, "What is it?"

"An observation rig," Elektra replied. "Travels inside

the pipe looking for broken seals. It performs all kinds of tasks, much like a robot. It runs automatically, but there's nothing scheduled—"

"Shut it down," Bond said.

A technician flicked two switches. The light continued to flash. Confused, he tried others, but there was no change. "I don't understand," he said. "It won't respond."

Christmas Jones appeared next to them. "The place is clean. There's no sign of—"

"The bomb is in the pipeline," Bond said, cutting her off.

"My God," Elektra said.

All eyes followed the route from the flashing light to the large mass of animated derricks on the eastern end of the map.

Robinson announced what they all realized simultaneously. "It's headed for the oil terminal."

"Where it can do the most damage," Bond said. "Elektra, have your men evacuate that terminal."

She bristled at him. "*Now* do you believe me?"

The look on Bond's face revealed his inner struggle. Was she right?

Elektra turned to the technician. "Do it. Tell them to evacuate, then clear this room." The man immediately got on the phone.

Bond looked at M. "He's going for the oil."

"Of course," M said, studying the map. "The one pipeline the West is counting on to supply our reserves for the next century."

The doubt in Bond's mind still nagged him. "But why? What's in it for him?"

M shrugged. "Revenge, as you say? Who knows, with a man like Renard? Chaos follows him wherever he goes. Do you have an idea?"

"Maybe," Bond replied, studying the map. He turned to another technician. "How far is that rig from the terminal? And how fast is it traveling?"

The man checked his readouts before replying. "It's a hundred and six miles from the terminal. Going seventy miles an hour."

"We've got less than ninety minutes," Bond said, thinking quickly. If he could get into the pipeline in *front* of the rig with the bomb, he just might be able to jump aboard and take care of the weapon. "Is there another rig?"

"There are several stored at random locations throughout the pipeline." The technician flipped a switch and another light blinked on the pipe map. "There's one parked in the same passageway. Ahead of it."

Perfect. Bond turned to Robinson. "Can you get me out there? Fast?"

Before Robinson could say yes, Christmas cut in. "Wait a minute. Are you going to try to do what I think you're going to try to do?"

"What do I need to defuse a nuclear bomb?" Bond asked.

"Me," she said smugly.

11

Pressure in the Pipeline

The Eurocopter swooped along the pipeline until it came to the nearest access hatch from the parked observation rig. The chopper set down and Bond, Christmas, and Robinson jumped out. Bond and Robinson turned the wheel on the hatch and got it open. Christmas, wearing a backpack full of tools, went in first. Bond followed.

"I'll be waiting to hear from you," Robinson told Bond, handing him a radio. "Good luck."

The light from the open hatch illuminated the circular tunnel just enough for Bond and Christmas to find their way a few meters in, where they found the rig. It was red and ring-shaped, resembling a doughnut on wheels, with two seats and a storage area for equipment and heavy objects. The thing was filthy with grease and dirt.

"You take the controls," Bond said as they climbed aboard. "We've got to get up to speed before the other rig catches us." He glanced at his watch. "I'm guessing we only have a few minutes. Do you know how to drive this thing?"

She examined the sparse control panel. There were only two toggle switches: "on/off" and "forward/reverse."

"It doesn't exactly take a degree in nuclear physics," she replied. She flipped the on button and the rig lurched forward. It was slow moving at first, but it gradually picked up speed on its own. The headlamps adequately lit the dark tunnel ahead of them, but there was something about the ride that was decidedly like a carnival haunted-house attraction. Bond half expected a fake skeleton to jump out and frighten them.

"Is there a way to make it go faster?" Bond asked.

"Not that I can see," she said. "It just gains speed on its own. Unless someone at the control center stops it or we manually throw it into reverse, I imagine it'll get up to sixty or seventy miles an hour pretty soon."

Bond looked behind them but saw nothing but darkness. There were no taillights on the rig.

"It won't be long before we hear it," she said. "Can you hear anything?"

"Not yet."

They both involuntarily gripped the sides of the noisy, clattering cart as they sat silently in anticipation and watched the speedometer rise from thirty to forty miles per hour. At one point, Christmas glanced over at Bond and studied his face in the dim light. He was certainly handsome, she thought.

She was beginning to appreciate the unfortunate circumstances that had brought them together.

Elektra and M stood together in the pipeline control room, anxiously watching the map on the wall. M's bodyguard, Gabor, and two of Elektra's men hovered a discreet distance away.

"Bond is in the pipeline," a technician announced. "And Mr. Robinson is on the way back."

They watched as the two blips on the map moved along the course. The one with the bomb was traveling faster; it wouldn't be long before it caught up with the second rig.

M thought that her harshness with Double-O Seven had been premature. Although he had disobeyed orders and left Elektra alone, he had discovered information that saved their lives. And here he was again risking his life to avert a horrible catastrophe. He certainly had courage . . . unless, of course, he was just trying to save face for suspecting Elektra King of killing her father. What nonsense!

She watched the young woman to see how she responded under pressure. Elektra was standing in front of the map, gnawing on a thumbnail. She had become very quiet since Bond left.

While they were waiting, the police officer in charge of the investigation made a preliminary report to Elektra. Renard's strike had caused a great deal of damage.

"From what we can fathom," he said, "four or five

men armed with automatic weapons attacked the site. It was meticulously planned, for the gang carried it off in less than an hour. During that time they killed two security guards and three technicians. Plastic explosives took out the electricity and crippled the site vehicles. They also got hold of an observation rig."

"They wired it so that it couldn't be shut off from the control center," a technician said.

"Mmm," the officer continued. "They apparently placed the bomb in the rig and sent it toward its destination. Upon leaving, they set the control room on fire."

"Thank you, Detective," Elektra said. "I'd appreciate it if your men leave us alone now. We're in a bit of a crisis. I'll be in touch soon, all right?"

"Yes, ma'am," the officer said. Elektra King apparently had a lot of authority, even over the local police. He quickly gathered his men and left the control room. Now M was completely alone with her bodyguard, Elektra, Gabor and his men, and a few technicians.

Without a hint of underlying defensiveness, M approached Elektra and offered an apology by way of explaining, "If there's even the slightest chance, Bond will succeed." She paused, then added, "He's the best we have."

Elektra replied noncommittally, "I hope you're right."

M continued to watch the blips on the map. A thought occurred to her that she hadn't considered. *How did Renard and his men know how to use the observation rig? Did they have help from someone in King Industries?*

She looked around the control room and wondered if

anyone standing nearby might be the insider who had switched King's lapel pin. Elektra's bodyguard? One of the technicians?

M suddenly began to feel uneasy. She hoped Robinson would hurry back.

Meanwhile, M16's best and Christmas Jones waited expectantly for the other rig to catch up with them. The speedometer on their rig read "50 mph." Finally, a whooshing noise interrupted the tense silence. Lights reflected on a bend. They looked behind them and saw the bomb-laden rig tearing through the pipe.

"Faster!" Bond cried. "Get our speed up!"

Christmas pressed forward, as if leaning against the dash would make the rig go faster.

"There's not a damned thing I can do about it!" she called.

Bond got in the back of the vehicle and extended his legs out toward the approaching rig. Its rumbling echoed louder in the tunnel as the lights came closer . . . closer . . .

Their vehicle jolted as the other rig made contact. Bond cushioned the blow with his feet as best he could, then held his legs straight against the front of the rig in an attempt to slow it down. He waited a moment until the other rig was traveling at a steady speed behind them, then he carefully climbed over onto it.

"Give me your hand!" he shouted. He helped Christmas across, but just as she shifted her weight onto the second rig, her foot slid off the surface and she almost fell between the two cars. Bond caught her shoulders just in time and hauled her up.

"Whew, thanks," she said. Once they were safely in, both rigs were traveling together at the same speed. The ride, however, was extremely bumpy.

Christmas went straight for the bomb, which was sitting in the rig bed, daunting and deadly. She removed her backpack, took out some tools, and examined the bomb. She attached a handheld computer the size of a transistor radio to some terminals on the device's LED panel and made some quick calculations

"It's a tactical fission device. Low yield," she said.

"How do we stop it?"

"*We,* Dr. *Arkov?* Move over. Hold me steady."

"You've defused hundreds of these, right?"

"Yeah. But they're usually standing still."

Bond smiled ironically and said, "Life is filled with small challenges."

She shot him a look, then set to work. Bond put his hands on her waist to help steady her. She didn't protest. The timer on the bomb read "1:45 Minutes" and the seconds were ticking down.

"Less than two minutes?" Bond asked, surprised. "The thing will go off before it arrives at the oil terminal. Did they make a mistake setting the timer?"

Christmas used a screwdriver to remove a plate.

. . . 1:30 . . .

"I don't know . . ." she said, concentrating, "but I sure don't want it blowing up in our faces, do you?"

She clipped wires inside the warhead.

. . . 1:20 . . .

"Look." Bond pointed to the sphere that contained the core. "Those screws. The heads are stripped."

"Somebody's tampered with the bomb," she agreed. "The core's been removed and put back in. That's weird."

She reached into her pack for the core extraction tool, but just at that instant the rig shot down a dip in the pipeline track. Christmas almost flew off, but Bond saved her by yanking the tool in her hand and pulling her back in. They exchanged sighs of relief then she set back to work.

"They need seat belts in these things," she said.

As the rig sped through the tunnel, Christmas manipulated the extraction tool to carefully lift the plutonium core from the sphere. It took longer than Bond had hoped.

. . . 0:55 . . .

"Look at this!" she said, surprised. The thing looked mangled. "Half the plutonium core is missing."

Bond opened a plastic bag for her. She dropped the core inside.

"So it won't go nuclear?"

"Yeah," she said. "But there's still enough explosive in the casing to kill both of us if the trigger charge goes off." He closed the bag and put it in the backpack.

. . . 0:44 . . .

"Don't worry, I can defuse it in time," she said. Bond's mind raced as he peered around the ghostly tunnel. Christmas continued to work.

. . . 0:40 . . .

It was very mysterious . . . the timer had been set to

go off *before* reaching the oil terminal . . . half of the plutonium was missing so that the bomb would only do minimal damage to the pipeline . . .

"Let it blow," he said suddenly.

About to snip a wire, she looked up, astonished. "But I can stop it."

"I said let it blow."

She couldn't believe what he was saying. His eyes shot to an inspection hatch that was illuminated by tunnel lights up ahead.

"Trust me. Leave it." He grabbed her and wrenched her away from the bomb. "Get ready to jump."

"Jump? Jump where?"

As the rigs zoomed past the exit hatch, Bond leaped off, taking her with him. They tumbled along the pipe, choking for a moment in the dust left by the two vehicles. Bond sprang to his feet, pulled her up, and then they ran like hell for the hatch.

. . . 0:10 . . .

The wheel on the hatch was stuck. Bond used every bit of his strength to budge it. *Come on, damn it!* he screamed in his head.

. . . 0:05 . . .

It creaked and turned! They got it open and climbed out just as the bomb exploded, demolishing a section of the pipe. Debris rocketed in every direction. They felt the force in the ground beneath them as they rolled away from the hatch and lay facedown with their hands covering their heads.

● ● ●

Back in the pipeline control centre, red concentric circles pulsed outward from the point of impact on the map. A monotone beep echoed in the large room. Everyone was frozen and shocked. Gabor had a radio to his ear, listening intently to Robinson, who was flying over the site. The others looked at him in anticipation. Finally, he nodded.

"The bomb was a dud," he said. "But the triggering charge blew out a fifty-yard section of pipe."

"How bad is the damage?" Elektra asked.

He shrugged. "Difficult to say at this point."

"And Bond?" M asked.

The alarm beep sputtered and died.

"Nothing," Gabor replied.

M couldn't hide the crestfallen expression on her face. After a moment, Elektra stepped to her and said, "I'm so sorry."

M nodded curtly.

Then, with a hint of a smile, Elektra continued, "But I have a gift for you."

M blinked, thinking this was an odd thing to say.

"Something that belonged to my father," Elektra said. "He would have wanted you to have it."

"Perhaps this isn't the time . . ." M began.

"Please."

She placed a small box in M's hand and untied the ribbon for her.

"He often spoke of how . . . compassionately you advised him on the best course of action during my kidnapping," she said.

M opened the box. Inside was the original Eye of the Glens lapel pin.

"It's very valuable, you know," Elektra said. "I just couldn't let it explode with the rest of him."

M was horrified.

Elektra gave a small nod to Gabor, who drew his gun and shot M's bodyguard at point-blank range. The man's chest exploded in a mass of red tissue. The other men surrounded M and aimed rifles at her.

M's only reaction was to give Elektra a bloodcurdling glare. So Bond's instincts were on target after all. The change in Elektra's demeanor was as horrifying as it was thorough. She was no longer the frightened victim, the helpless daughter . . . Now she was back in control, a harpy with blood in her eyes.

"You advised my father not to pay the ransom," she said. "M16 . . . the great protector of the free world. And I thought you were like family, M. You were more interested in catching your terrorist than freeing me. And my *father* went along with it!"

"We would have freed you with a little more time," M said.

"Oh, that's rich," Elektra spat. "After I'd been raped and treated like an animal for three weeks? I was terribly upset when the money bomb didn't kill both of you," she said to M. "I didn't think I'd get another chance. Then you dropped the answer right in my lap. Your man Bond. It was so easy to use him to lure you here, just as you used me during my kidnapping. How does it feel? How does it feel to know that he was right about me after all? As you say, he's the best you have. Or should I say *had*?"

M slapped her hard. The men lunged and restrained her.

Elektra rubbed her cheek lightly but otherwise revealed no emotion.

"Take her to the helicopter," she ordered the men.

Gabor and another man took hold of M's upper arms, but she roughly shrugged them off. Still glaring at the girl who had betrayed her, M held her head high and marched out of the room with her captors.

Renard received the call en route to Istanbul in Truhkin's Land Rover.

"It's done," Elektra said. "Your plan was brilliant."

He breathed a sigh of relief. It was good to hear her voice. "And what about Bond?"

"You won't be hearing from him. He was killed in the pipeline, trying to stop your bomb."

"That's excellent news," he said.

"I have another surprise for you when I see you," she said. "When will you arrive in Istanbul?" He was glad that she sounded so happy.

"It won't be long," he said. "Hurry. I want to see you."

"We're on our way."

Renard rang off and turned to Truhkin. "Are you sure you know what to do with the plutonium we took?"

"Sure, no problem," said the Russian. "We mold it into the shape of a rod with the extruder. I'll use the dimensions that your man provided."

"How long will it take?"

"A few minutes once we have the extruder. As soon as we get to Istanbul, I'll start work. Are you sure the extruder will be there?"

"Don't worry, it's coming," Renard said.

He was satisfied. Renard tried to relax as Truhkin drove, then glanced back at the heavy shielded case that was carrying their half core of plutonium. Inside was the future of the world, he thought. At last, he was going to be a part of it. All his life he had attempted to make a difference . . . fighting for causes he believed in, inciting others to commit violence in his name, forcing governments to listen to him . . .

In two days, he would be dead, but Renard took comfort in the knowledge that his love would live on through the woman he was doing all this for. Some might say that it was hatred that was responsible for the destruction and loss of life that would result from his coming actions.

To hell with what they thought.

This was about love.

Bond and Christmas sat in the dirt, catching their breath. The sun beat down on them. The ruptured, smoldering break in the pipeline was not far away.

"Do you want to explain why you did that?" she asked. "I could've stopped that bomb. You almost killed us."

"I did kill us," Bond said. "She thinks we're dead. And she thinks she got away with it."

"Do you want to put that in English? For those of us who don't speak 'spy'? Who is 'she'?"

"Elektra King."

"Elektra King? This is *her* pipeline! Why would she want to blow it up?"

Bond shrugged. "Makes her look even more innocent." He knew he was right, but he didn't know the whole story yet. He began to think aloud. "It's part of some plan. They steal a bomb. Put it in the pipeline . . ."

"But why leave half the plutonium?" Christmas asked, holding up the bag containing the half-grapefruit-sized piece of material.

Bond's mind clicked. "So there'd be just enough spread around in the blast to cover up for the half they took."

"But what are they going to do with it?"

"You're the nuclear scientist. You tell me."

"I don't know," she said, thinking. "It's not enough to make a bomb. But . . . Whatever we do, we have to get that plutonium back. I'm responsible for that testing centre in Kazakhstan. Somebody's going to have *my* ass for this."

"First things first." Bond flicked on the radio. "Bond to Robinson. Do you read?"

The radio's response was nothing but static.

Christmas took the opportunity to ask, "By the way . . . Were you and Elektra . . . like . . . ?"

Bond gave her a disapproving look, but she continued, "I mean, before we go any further, I just want to know. What's the story with you two?"

Bond wasn't about to answer. "Bond to Robinson.

Come in!" Then, to turn the tables on Christmas, he asked, "What's yours? What were *you* doing in Kazakhstan?"

She nailed him with her answer. "Avoiding those kinds of questions. Just like you."

Bond was about to say "touché," when the radio crackled.

"I read you, Double-O Seven," Robinson said. "Red alert. M is missing. Her bodyguard is dead. The pipeline control center has been evacuated. The King Industries helicopter is missing, and Elektra King is nowhere in sight. We don't know where they are. Awaiting instructions. Out."

Bond closed his eyes. A bad situation had just become worse. Christmas was horrified. Bond's face grew grim as he masked his feelings and looked off at the pipeline. She knew enough not to probe.

"What do we do now?" she asked.

A thought struck Bond. "There's one critical element here I may have overlooked. We have to track it down."

"What? More plutonium?"

"No," Bond said. "Beluga. *Caviar.*"

12
Prisoner of the Past

The Bosphorus, the twenty-mile-long strait that connects the Black Sea with the Sea of Marmara, is the source of many tales. Jason, of Greek myth fame, sailed the ship *Argo* from the Aegean Sea, through the Bosphorus, and into the Black Sea in search of the Golden Fleece. As they are the only outlet for the Black Sea, the waterways have, from the beginnings of recorded history, served as migration or invasion routes for the peoples of Europe and Asia. The Bosphorus has always been a strategic focal point in the magnificent city of Istanbul, the link between the two continents. The western shore lies in Europe, while the eastern one is in Asia. The hilly shores on both sides are scattered with castles and extravagant villas—vestiges of the region's vivid past—as well as the more modern beach resorts that cater to leisure-seeking citizens of Istanbul.

The Kiz Kulesi, also known as "Leander's Tower" or "Maiden's Tower," is one such ancient monument, located on a tiny islet near the Asian shore. According to legend, a Turkish princess was once confined to the islet by her father, who had learned from a prophecy that his beloved child would die of snakebite and believed he could avoid the fate by hiding her away. Nevertheless, the princess met her fate on the islet, for a snake that had been smuggled in from the mainland eventually bit her. The English name "Leander" was given to the tower out of the mistaken belief that the legendary figure Leander drowned in its vicinity when he tried to swim the strait to meet his lover.

In actuality, a Byzantine emperor had the tower built in the twelfth century. With a chain strung just below the waterline from the tower to Sarayburnu, or Seraglio Point, the emperor could close the Bosphorus to all incoming or outgoing vessels.

At twilight, a boat put in at the Kiz Kulesi. King Industries had leased the monument as an Istanbul office and very few people knew that the old place was occupied. Plans had been formulated to open it up to tourists, but for the monument, the Maiden's Tower appeared to be a neglected, derelict building.

Renard the Fox disembarked from the boat followed by several of his retinue, heavily laden with bags and cases. They entered the tower, an extraordinary space with stained-glass windows that cast myriad patterns over elaborate tile and marble surfaces. Pillars, iron lattice, velvet drapes, and flowers covered the huge room. It was like entering a museum.

"At last!" Elektra King swooped across the floor into Renard's arms. He embraced her passionately.

She moaned as he squeezed her tightly. Then she pushed him away. "You're hurting me," she said. "You don't know your own strength."

Renard hadn't expected such a cold response. He let her go as he studied her face, sensing something was now different between them. Whatever it was, he could see that she was attempting to hide it by acting flirtatious. "Brought me something?"

He smiled, grabbed a case off one of his men, and opened it.

"The power to reshape the world," he said.

He pulled out a sphere of cobalt-blue metal. She gazed at it with a wary fascination.

"Go on," he said. "It's safe. Touch your destiny."

She traced a finger along the metal.

"Warm," she observed with a flicker of wonder.

"Is it?" A dark cloud passed over his face. The half smile vanished. After an awkward moment, he said, "I have to get it to the boys. They're going to reshape it into a rod."

"I've brought something for you as well," Elektra said, sensing his frustration and wishing to alleviate it. "Remember I said I had a surprise for you?"

She opened a heavy door and led Renard through a passageway into a small room. An area filled with antique pottery, statues, and other works of ancient art was set apart from the rest of the room by a wall of bars, creating a kind of cell. The area contained another occupant as well: a very defiant-looking M.

"Your present," Elektra announced. "Courtesy of the late Mr. Bond."

Renard stepped forward and peered through the bars at the woman, who appeared tired, but was otherwise in good shape.

"Well, well. My executioner," he said.

"Overpraise, I'm afraid," M said. "But my people will finish the job."

"Your people?" Elektra asked. "Your people will leave you here to rot—just like you left me. You and my father . . . who didn't think my life was worth the money he threw away on a bad night in the casino."

"Your father wasn't—"

"My father was nothing!" Elektra proclaimed with an uncharacteristically shrill note in her voice. M could see that the young woman had obviously turned a corner in her emotional life. Now that the masquerade was over, the poor girl had completely lost touch with reality.

"My father's kingdom he stole from my mother!" she cried. "The kingdom that I will rightly take back." With that, she turned on her heels and left the room. Renard was left alone with M.

The head of SIS turned to her captor, anger blazing in her eyes. "I hope you're proud of what you did to her," she said.

"I'm afraid you're the one who deserves credit." He tried to smile again, the gruesome half face a *commedia dell'arte* mask in the dim light of the cell. "When I took her she was . . . promise itself. And you left her at the mercy of a man like me. Three weeks is a long time. Her father could have paid the ransom and she would never have been . . . corrupted. *You* ruined her. For what? To get to me? She's worth fifty of me."

"For once I agree with you," M said, her eyes as cold as steel.

He shook his head, amused by her pluck. "Yes. And now we also share a common fate."

He took a small travel clock out of his pocket, checked the time on his wristwatch, and set the clock.

"Since you sent your man to murder me, I've been watching time tick slowly away, marching toward my own death. And now you'll have the same pleasure. Watch these hands, M. At noon tomorrow, your time is up. And I guarantee you: I will not miss. You *will* die. Along with everyone in this city and the bright, starry, oil-driven future of the West."

He placed the clock on a tall stool just out of reach through the bars. He then looked M up and down, and left the room.

M stared in horror at the clock, which read "8:00 P.M."

An hour later, Renard and Elektra were in her bedroom in the tower. She was naked, lying facedown, as he stroked her slowly, worshiping her skin. The tension he had sensed earlier was still present. She had hardly said a word to him.

"So beautiful," he whispered. "So smooth, so warm."

"How would you know?" she said cruelly.

He was stung by her allusion to his affliction and pulled back. "Why are you like this?" he asked. "What's the matter with you?"

"I don't know."

"Don't lie to me. It's Bond, isn't it?"

"What?"

"Is it because Bond is dead?"

She set her jaw and was silent.

Renard was flustered. "It's what you wanted!"

Elektra hesitated again. Angry now, Renard leaped up and paced the floor. She sat up and pulled a silk robe around her.

"Of course it's what I wanted," she said, trying to salve his feelings.

He turned to confront her. "He was a . . . good lover?"

"What do you think? That I wouldn't feel anything?"

Renard leaned against her desk and closed his eyes, attempting to squeeze out the images. After a moment, he smashed his fist through the hand-painted wood. At the sound of her gasp, he looked at his hand. A huge splinter of wood was stuck in it. He looked at it inquisitively.

"Nothing," he said. "I don't feel a damned thing." It was almost a whimper.

Elektra moved to him, took him by the arm, and led him back to the bed. She gently pulled out the splinter, then reached into the ice bucket on the floor. She ran a piece of ice along the wound.

"What about this?" she asked.

She moved the ice on his cheek. He shook his head, tormented.

"Nothing."

Then she rubbed the ice down her own neck. Water dribbled down between her breasts. "But surely . . ." Her fingers were wet now, and she touched and aroused herself with the ice-cold liquid. ". . . You can feel this?"

She moved the ice lower. Her lips opened as she clearly enjoyed the sensation. The half smile on Renard's face grew as she continued to arouse herself.

"Remember . . . pleasure?" she asked sensually.

They made love, if that's what one could call it. Renard found his pleasure, to be sure, although it wasn't by any traditional means. For her part, Elektra submitted to her desire for the man who was once her tormentor. She was a prisoner of her past, but for once, she was the one in control.

It was still later, as they lay naked together in each other's arms, when the phone rang. She stirred from the postcoital feeling of letdown and answered it.

"Yes?" She listened as Renard's one closed eye flicked open. "I see. Thank you." She hung up and said, "Bond is alive. He's in Baku."

Baku's "City of Walkways," a network of raised boardwalks and platforms constructed over the water near the shoreline, is a curious structure that provides docking areas for boats, as well as storage facilities, shops, bars, and brothels for the seamen, fishermen, and petroleum workers. It is square-shaped but spiral, in construction, like a multistory car park, with the lower levels connecting to the upper ones by means of slanted bridges. At first glance, the place resembles an M. C. Escher drawing of a labyrinth, with walkways and bridges connecting here and there with no apparent rhyme or reason. In fact, it was practically and ingeniously designed long ago by using the boardwalks for support as well as walkways. These were now littered with petrol cans, crates of fresh fish, forgotten pieces of machinery, and other odoriferous items, but the strongest smell in the air was that of petroleum.

Valentin Zukovsky's Rolls-Royce pulled up to the peculiar structure, where his caviar factory sat on the top level. Guards piled out of the back and opened the door for him. Wearing a tuxedo, Zukovsky, got out and scanned the horizon.

"Wait here," he said to the men.

He limped toward the structure of walkways and his factory, using a silver cane. *Why had Dmitri, the foreman, insisted that he come down to the factory immediately?* he wondered. *What was the big crisis?* "It's always something," he mumbled to himself. "First it's the casino. Then it's the factory. I'm a slave to the free-market economy . . ."

Zukovsky's chauffeur, The Bull, sat in the Rolls and watched his boss enter the building. His sharp eyes continued to survey the surroundings, looking for anything unusual. He raised his eyebrows when he saw the BMW Z8 parked behind a billboard in an obvious attempt to hide it from sight.

The Bull punched some numbers on his cell phone, making a call to Elektra King in Istanbul. After the exchange, he looked at his watch. It was time. He pulled the AK-47 from beneath the seat, held it under his jacket, and got out of the car.

Zukovsky paused at the door of his fishery to admire—and straighten—a sign bearing his likeness—ZUKOVSKY'S FINEST—WORLDWIDE HEADQUARTERS. He opened the door, stepped inside, and found himself staring down the barrel of a Walther PPK.

James Bond was holding Dmitri, a short man dressed in a caviar factory smock, by the collar. The man looked helpless and apologetic. Christmas Jones stood by, watching with interest.

Zukovsky sighed. "Couldn't you just say hello?"

Bond released the foreman. "Beat it," he ordered. "Out the back." Dmitri scampered off, leaving Bond with his gun aimed at Zukovsky's rather bulbous nose.

"Now then," Bond said. "What's your business with Elektra King?"

"I thought *you* were the one giving her the business," Zukovsky replied. He looked over at Christmas and smiled. She seemed to be a bit taken aback by the look on his face.

Bond continued. "She dropped a million dollars in your casino—and you didn't even blink. What was she paying you off for?"

"I don't know what you're talking about, Bond-JamesBond."

"The million-dollar chit which you so easily won with a rigged card deck. It was a payoff for services rendered. What were they?"

Zukovsky glanced at Christmas again. "If I were you . . . a relationship with this guy? Don't bet on it."

With his free arm, Bond slammed Zukovsky against a vat of caviar. Wood split and roe spilled all over the floor.

Zukovsky was appalled. "That is five thousand dollars of Beluga! Ruined!"

"Nothing compared to what a twenty-megaton nuclear bomb would do."

"What are you talking about?"

The sound of an approaching helicopter outside didn't deter Bond from pressing the gun against Zukovsky's temple.

"I work for the IDA," Christmas said. "We had a nuclear bomb stolen—"

Bond cut her off. "Renard and Elektra are working together."

Zukovsky looked genuinely surprised and somewhat shocked. "I didn't know!" he pleaded.

"What *do* you know?"

Zukovsky was about to answer when there was a loud crash. Wood splintered everywhere as the wall and roof tore open behind them. Zukovsky's jaw dropped as they saw a Eurocopter "Squirrel" armed with giant, vertically suspended circular saws rip through his shop.

Bond pushed Christmas and the Russian to safety, the spinning teeth barely missing them. The blades churned through the roof, spraying caviar everywhere.

Bond burst out of the building, pushing Zukovsky and Christmas ahead of him. Zukovsky's guards were already firing at the helicopter. Zukovsky produced a TEC DC-9 semiautomatic handgun from inside his jacket and sprayed bullets into the air. Unfortunately, the helicopter kept coming, its deadly saws ripping everything in sight and making a deafening noise.

Within moments, The Bull was there with his AK-47. He made a show of firing at the helicopter but deliberately missed.

"Get back inside!" Bond yelled to Christmas and Zukovsky. They were no better off out there. As they ran back into the demolished factory, Bond made for the BMW, running down a flight of steps onto a lower walkway. Before he could make it to the landing, a grenade was thrown from a second Squirrel that appeared above him. It, too, was armed with the bizarre circular saws that hung below the aircraft. The grenade blew out the section of the walkway in front of Bond, knocking him back.

The fire and smoke trapped him. The only way out was along the pipelines. He ran beside a narrow section of pipe, then jumped down to another walkway. The pipes were now above him, but the second chopper's relentless saws cut through them, releasing gas. Bond hurled himself up a stairway to get out of the way.

Inside the factory, Zukovsky and Christmas watched in horror as the first helicopter continued to slice away more of the roof above them. As they ran for cover, Zukovsky yelled to her, "I told you he was a bad bet!"

Bond found himself on a ramp leading to the platform where the BMW was parked. He removed the remote-control device from his pocket and pressed buttons. The BMW roared to life, pulled out from behind the billboard, and drove toward him, driverless. He rushed to meet it as the second chopper followed, slicing up the walkway behind him. He jumped into the passenger's seat just as the helicopter veered away.

Now feeling that he had something of a chance, Bond activated the missiles as he watched the helicopter pass behind the factory. Then there was a horrible screeching sound as the car lurched. The first helicopter's blades ripped through the roof of the BMW, cutting it in half lengthwise.

"You'll answer to Q for that," Bond muttered, then pressed the button to fire a missile. A grille on the side of the car flipped open and a foot-long heat-seeking missile slid out on a track. The missile's fins unfolded and the weapon shot off toward the target.

It was a direct hit. The first helicopter exploded and pieces of it fell onto the walkway. Because of the broken gas pipes, the entire area was set ablaze.

Zukovsky and Christmas went out from the back of the factory, only to see the second chopper drop four armed men onto a nearby walkway. They began to fire at Zukovsky's guards as they ran toward the factory. Zukovsky sheltered Christmas and returned fire.

"Tell me what you know!" Christmas yelled.

"Later, woman!" Zukovsky shouted back. "I'm fighting for capitalism!"

Bond jumped out of the disabled vehicle and ran back toward the factory. He could see that the others were under attack. The second helicopter was hot on his tail, though, and the men inside opened fire. Bond zigzagged along the walkway, intent on depriving them of an easy target. He managed to outrun the gunfire, but a grenade exploded ahead of him, destroying the walkway and hurling him into the water.

The armed men successfully took out Zukovsky's guards and moved even closer to the couple.

"Back! Now! Move!" Zukovsky shouted, pushing Christmas back into the factory.

Two of the assailants followed them. The Bull was inside, blasting away with his own gun. The bullets cut the air over Zukovsky's head as he held Christmas down behind a table. In the heat of the battle, neither of them noticed that none of the gunfire was being directed at The Bull.

Suddenly Bond burst through a trapdoor in the floor between them and the gunmen. Before the two men realized what had happened, Bond shot them.

The place was on fire now. "Get out of here!" he shouted to his friends. He saw a third gunman lurking in the basement below and shot him as Zukovsky pulled Christmas off the floor and ran outside.

The pair made it to the Rolls and jumped in. Zukovsky rammed the car into reverse just as the helicopter sliced the boardwalk to smithereens behind him. Christmas screamed. Zukovsky was unable to stop. The car flew backward into the water.

Inside the burning factory, Bond had engaged the remaining gunmen in a furious gunfight. He had to stop once to replace his magazine, and this pause in the action must have given the assailants a false sense of victory. One of them rose from his cover to see if Bond was dead. Bond shot him between the eyes. A barrage of bullets came from the last man, but Bond rolled over a burning ember and got the man in his sight. Two bullets knocked him into oblivion. Before leaving the disaster area, Bond noticed a flare gun mounted on the wall. He grabbed it, then ran outside.

He looked around feverishly for Christmas and Zukovsky and finally heard them splashing in the water. They were swimming to safety, but the helicopter was still hovering above them and shooting. Bond jumped down to a boardwalk at water level and cranked open a gas jet. He stood on the platform and waved at the pilot, daring the helicopter to come at him. He waited for the chopper to line up over the gas jet, then he fired the flare gun. The gas ignited and shot up to engulf the helicopter in an immense fireball. Debris from the aircraft flew everywhere.

Zukovsky pulled himself back onto a walkway and headed for the factory, but two free-flying saw blades from the chopper were sailing right at him. He dived to the side, directly into a caviar pit. The saws stuck into the cabin behind him.

The caviar pit was like quicksand. Zukovsky slowly started to sink, trying to cling to a crate blown in there by the explosion.

Bond and Christmas appeared, soaking wet. "Now . . . where were we?" Bond asked the blubbering Russian, who was at the point of being swallowed by the caviar, clawing at the crate.

"A rope! Please!" he shouted.

"No. The truth," Bond said coldly. "Those blades were meant for you, Valentin. What do you know that she wants you dead for?"

"I'm drowning! Please!"

Bond turned to Christmas. "What's the atomic weight of caviar?"

"Probably close to cesium . . . He seems to have negative buoyancy," she replied.

"So he *will* drown."

"Sooner, rather than later."

"Stop it!" Zukovsky cried. "Get me out of here!"

"Too bad we don't have any champagne," Bond said.

"Or sour cream," she said, stifling a giggle.

"All right! All right!" the Russian yelled. "Sometimes I buy machinery for her. Russian stuff."

"And the payoff on the tables?"

"A special job. My nephew's in the navy. He's smuggling some equipment for her."

"Where?"

"No! Get me out!"

"Not yet. What's the destination?"

"This is a family matter!" Zukovsky pleaded. "If Nikolai is in danger, we do it my way, or nothing!"

Bond didn't move. The Russian sank deeper.

"Okay!" he yelled. "Istanbul! Now get me out!"

Bond pondered this for a moment; then he grabbed Zukovsky's cane and slammed one end down into the caviar for him to grab. Some of the stuff splattered on his jacket. He wiped it off with his index finger, then tasted it.

"Excellent quality, Valentin," he said. "My compliments."

At that moment the Bull burst into the room, ready to fire his gun. When he saw that it was only the three of them, he relaxed, then helped Bond get Zukovsky out of the pit. Zukovsky plopped down onto the floor, gasping.

"Now," Bond said. "Let's go and find your nephew."

13

The Maiden's Tower

I t was just after midnight.

Renard stood on a balcony in the Maiden's Tower, looking out over the Bosphorus with binoculars. Beyond the iron balustrades was one of the most fabulous views in the world. On one side were the still waters of the Golden Horn, and on the other were the dancing waves of the unsheltered Bosphorus. In between were the tumbling roofs, soaring minarets, and crouching mosques of the Pera district of Istanbul.

A supertanker had just entered the strait and was chugging along toward a port somewhere on the European side. Beneath its belly, however, hugging the tanker's shadow, was another vessel that had sneaked into the Bosphorus undetected.

It was a Russian Charlie II–class nuclear submarine. Officially designated as an SSGN, a nuclear-guided cruise-missile submarine, this class of boat was possibly the oldest of its type still retained by Russia. Compared with newer submarines, it was relatively noisy, but it was known to pack a powerful punch with a battery of eight SS-N-9 Siren antiship missiles and six 533 mm torpedo tubes with twelve weapons. Submerged, it could travel at twenty-four knots, powered by a pressurized water reactor with steam turbines driving one five-bladed screw and 15,000-shaft horsepower.

It was just what Renard was waiting for.

He flipped on the walkie-talkie. When Elektra answered, he said, "It's here."

"Right on schedule," she said.

"I'll make the necessary arrangements with the crew."

"It's in your hands, my dear."

He turned off the radio and peered through the binoculars once again. Then Renard felt something inside the wound on his temple. The bullet was moving again. There was no pain, just an uncomfortable sensation of pressure. *The damned thing is alive!* he thought wryly.

The doctor had warned him that should he begin to feel more movement in the area, it might mean that his time was nearly up. Renard knew he should seek medical help immediately, but the mission was too important. Besides, he had resigned himself to his fate.

He just hoped that time wouldn't run out before he completed his plan.

•   •   •

Deep within the tower, M paced her cell. According to the alarm clock outside her prison, she had twelve hours left. She was determined not to cooperate with her captors in any way, and she convinced herself that SIS would find her. If only she could think of a way to help Tanner and Robinson . . .

The stone dungeon had become chilly. She had worked up a sweat from pacing, no doubt losing some calories in the process, and now she was cold. She put on her jacket, which had been left draped around the only modern, wooden chair in the room. Other than that, she was left with a stone cot, a tin basin and water pitcher, a towel, a bucket, and dozens of useless antiques. They had allowed her to keep her handbag after going through it. Anything that could possibly be used as a weapon had been removed, and she was left with a set of keys, tissues, lipstick, and her passport. She had thought long and hard how she might make use of any one or more of these items. The pottery or a small statuette might work to smash over someone's head . . . the basin and jug were too light to be effective weapons . . . a towel could be used for strangling . . . She certainly wasn't afraid of fighting for her life if it came to that . . .

She buried her hands in her pockets and felt something odd in the right one. It was flat and rectangular, like a credit card. What was this?

M pulled it out and remembered. It was the locator card that Bond had given her. She was surprised that Elektra's men didn't find it, but she hadn't been wearing the jacket when they frisked her. They hadn't bothered to look!

She examined the locator card closely. It was plain, smooth, and silver plated, with two copper terminals at one end. She thought about this and what it might mean. Basically it was a homing device . . . with positive and negative terminals . . .

M looked at the clock.

Twelve-fourteen A.M.

She removed one of her high-heeled shoes and got down on the floor. She stuck the shoe out through the bars, extending her arm through them as far as it would go, and attempted to hook the stool's closest leg with the high heel. It was a strain; all she could do was tap the leg with the tip of the heel.

Right, she thought. *Let's lose a pound for another half inch* . . .

M squeezed her shoulder against the bars as hard as she could. It was painful, but she was able to get a better angle on the stool leg. She tapped it, this time dragging the stool slightly closer to her. *Tap . . . tap . . .* a little harden . . . *That's it.* She willed the stool to move . . . *tap . . . tap . . .*

Finally, she was able to hook the heel completely around the leg. She dragged the stool toward her, but the rickety thing hit a bump on the stone floor and spilled over. The clock hit the ground and skidded toward her, creating an awful noise that echoed in the stone chamber.

M heard scuffling outside the door. She quickly got up, hurried to the stone cot, and lay down.

Seconds later the keys rattled in the door and Gabor stuck his head inside. Not noticing the stool, he looked at the prisoner and the condition of her cell. M's eyes were closed and she was breathing heavily. Nothing seemed amiss. Satisfied, he shut the door behind him and locked it.

After waiting a moment, M scrambled back to the floor, reached out, and grabbed the clock. She opened the back and found two AA batteries. She took them out and set them on the stone cot. Next, she got her keys out of the handbag. She began to wedge the thinnest key into the top of one of the batteries. She chiseled until the terminal came off. She repeated the process with the other battery except that she levered off the opposite end.

Now all she had to do was connect the batteries to the copper terminals on the locator card and she just might be in business . . .

Elektra King shivered slightly and put on a silk robe. Unable to sleep, she decided that she might as well get up.

The maiden of the tower paced her bedroom, pausing every so often to look out the window at the night sky. In less than twelve hours, she thought, it would all be over. She would be safely back in England and would make a grief-stricken, compassionate statement to the media. She would pledge to do everything in her power to see that King Industries did its part in helping the world get back on its feet in the aftermath of the disaster.

Disaster . . .

It was a word that accurately described what was about to happen. She smiled wickedly at the thought. It was a brilliant plan! No one could possibly trace the catastrophe back to her. M would be dead. Her own people were loyal. It was too bad about Renard . . . but it was his choice to see the plan through to its deadly end. He didn't have long to live anyway. She would miss him, but he was insignificant in the grand scheme of things. She couldn't help it if the poor fool was in love with her. He had served his purpose. It would have been nice to have him around, but what with his head injury . . . and lack of feelings . . . he couldn't satisfy her now in the way that other men—men like James Bond—could. Elektra had never sorted out her feelings about Renard. On the one hand he had kidnapped her . . . on the other, they had shared an unparalleled intimacy . . .

And what about James Bond? He was the only unknown factor in all this. He was probably on his way to Istanbul. It had been wise of her to bring The Bull into her employ. Anyone could be bought, and he was no exception. The man with the gold teeth had his orders, so she put the M16 agent out of her head as best she could. James Bond would never find M in time. He would die along with millions of others.

Elektra reflected on this thought for a moment. Millions of people were going to die. It was a terrible thing. She clenched her fists and repeated to herself that millions of people had died over the centuries for all sorts of reasons. Besides, with the wealth that she would amass over the next ten years, she could rebuild the entire country.

Maybe they would even make her their ruler . . .

She gazed at the stars in the sky and thought of her

parents. *Well, father?* she silently asked. *What do you think of your "little princess" now? Are you proud? Have I not shown initiative? If only you could be here to see the new global order as dictated by your daughter. Elektra King . . . Queen of the World . . .* She liked the sound of that.

Then she heard it again . . . her mother's lullaby. It was floating in the distance, softly wafting over the waters of the Bosphorus. Elektra began to rock from side to side with the music, singing it to herself.

This is all for you, Mother, she thought. *I'm doing this for you. Aren't you proud of your little girl? Smile, Mother. Your daughter loves you.*

As if on cue, the first sliver of morning sunlight struck the dark sky.

Renard took several men to the quay that had been fashioned beneath the ancient arched underbelly of a waterside building attached to the tower. The structure had existed for centuries, designed to protect ships when they were docked at the islet. When King Industries took over the property, all they had to do was install lights, a dock with a platform, and steps, and they had a berth for a ship . . . or a submarine.

He looked at his watch: 12:30. A little late, but not too bad . . .

The long black shadow of the SSGN could be seen beneath the waves. A mass of bubbles appeared as the huge vessel began to rise. Finally, the fairwater broke the surface and the submarine came to a halt.

Renard and his men stepped down to the platform and

waited. After a moment, the hatch opened and a youthful captain emerged.

"Captain Nikolai . . ." Renard said.

"Sir," the captain replied. "Ready to load your cargo. We have only a few hours before we'll be missed."

"You came with a skeleton crew?"

"That's all we can afford these days!"

"Of course . . . We have brandy and refreshments for your men."

Nikolai beamed as two of Renard's men came forward with baskets of goods.

Renard was pleased. The deal Elektra had made with the captain's uncle had paid off. From what he knew of Valentin Zukovsky, the young captain bore a strong resemblance. The young Russian shared his uncle's thirst for money as well, for it didn't take a lot to persuade him to "borrow" the submarine from the navy for a few hours. After all, if the captain of a nuclear submarine decided to go on silent patrol, who was to stop him? It wasn't unusual for subs to be out of touch for a period of time.

Nikolai and his men would prove to be very useful indeed. They were strong, eager, and hungry. They would obey orders without question.

It was too bad they would all have to die.

Eski Istanbul, or the Old City, woke up to the dawn with the usual hustle and bustle of street vendors moving their carts into place at the Grand Bazaar. It is here where remnants of Turkey's colorful history manifest themselves in a single place. The Byzantine city of centuries past, it is in Eski that one finds the great palaces, mosques, hippodromes, churches, monumental columns, and markets.

Not far from the Grand Bazaar is a very old power station. It was closed down during the Second World War but was never demolished, supposedly for some historical reason. The locals generally ignored it, as if it wasn't there. The truth, as Valentin Zukovsky explained it to James Bond and Christmas Jones as they arrived after the overnight trip from Baku, was that it had served as a KGB safe house during the cold war.

"Now it's the FSS," he said. "Federal Security Services. Same old friendly service. New name."

The building was full of Soviet generators, outdated electric typewriters, and computers, copiers, and surveillance equipment ranging from ten to forty years old. Men and women were busy at various terminals as if the cold war had never ended.

Zukovsky led the couple to a radio operator. The Bull, carrying a brown briefcase, followed not far behind.

"Did you raise him?" Zukovsky asked.

"*Nyet.* Nothing," the operator replied.

"Try scanning the emergency frequencies," Bond suggested.

"Are you sure you have no clue what kind of cargo your nephew agreed to transport?" Christmas asked.

"No, I swear," Zukovsky said. "All I know is that he was being paid a million dollars, minus my commission, of course, to borrow a Russian navy boat, come to Istanbul from the Black Sea, and pick up some stuff. I have no idea what. He could get away with it, you see, because he is a captain."

They moved on to a large map of the Bosphorus and the Black Sea, complete with scattered multicolored pins.

Zukovsky sighed. "A tragedy. In the old days, we had a hundred places where a submarine could surface undetected."

Bond put a hand on Zukovsky's arm. "A submarine! Why didn't you tell us?"

Zukovsky shrugged. "Didn't I? I assumed you knew. My nephew is captain of a submarine."

"What class is your nephew running?"

"Charlie class . . ."

"Nuclear." It all came together for Bond. "Valentin, your nephew didn't borrow the boat to load cargo. Renard wants the sub itself." He looked at Christmas. "They want to use the reactor."

"That's it!" Christmas concurred. "You put weapons-grade plutonium in that sub's reactor and you get instant, catastrophic meltdown. The submarine becomes the bomb."

"And it's made to look like an accident," Bond said.

"But why?" Zukovsky asked.

He pointed to the map. "Because all of the existing pipelines from the Caspian Sea go to the north, to here— where the oil is put on tankers and shipped across the Black Sea to Istanbul. The explosion would destroy Istanbul, contaminating the Bosphorus for decades. There'd be only one way to get the oil out of the Caspian Sea."

"Through the south . . . the King pipeline," Christmas said.

"*Elektra's* pipeline."

The urgency of the situation finally hit home with Zukovsky. "We've got to find Nikolai and warn him!"

Suddenly the radio operator called, "I've got something!" and hurried over with a piece of paper. The Bull leaned in close to overhear what the man had to say.

"On the emergency frequency. Two six-digit numbers, cycled every fifteen seconds."

"A GPS signal," Christmas observed. The Global Positioning System could pinpoint the exact location of an object and was mostly used for navigation on the high seas. "What could that be?"

Bond had one of those rare *eureka!* moments. "It's M! The locator card! I gave it to her at the construction site. That's got to be her." He grabbed the paper and compared it with the big map. He pointed to the coordinates.

"Here."

"The Maiden's Tower," Zukovsky said. "Kiz Kulesi."

"Do you know it?" Bond asked.

He turned to Zukovsky, and out of the corner of his eye noticed The Bull slipping out the door. The brown briefcase he had been carrying was sitting on a chair.

"We used it during the Afghan War . . ." Zukovsky began, but Bond sensed something was very wrong. "It's a very old place," Zukovsky continued, "I think it was built in——"

But Bond didn't let him finish. "Bomb!" he shouted as he grabbed Christmas and pulled her behind the cover of some old generators just as a tremendous explosion ripped the place apart. In half a second, the air was thick with dust and smoke.

Coughing, Bond stood and waved the debris away. Christmas was stunned, but okay. Some in the room were dead, others knocked unconscious—including Zukovsky.

"Let's get out of here," Bond said to Christmas. He took her hand and rushed outside.

The street was clear, but smoke was pouring out of the building. A siren could be heard in the distance. They ran to the corner and rounded it, only to come face-to-face with Gabor and several heavily armed men.

On instinct, Bond reached for his gun, but he heard the sound of a round being chambered in a firearm directly behind him.

"Drop it," a familiar voice commanded.

Bond turned to see The Bull holding an AK-47. The chauffeur smiled coldly and added, "I insist."

"Of course you do," Bond said as Gabor and another man patted him and the girl down. Christmas looked at him as if to ask, "What now?" Bond looked back at her grimly.

At that moment, a black sedan screeched around the corner and stopped.

"We go for a ride now," Gabor said. "I'm sure Miss King would like to see you." He gave a high five to The Bull, then shoved his gun barrel into Bond's back.

"Your boss doesn't like to be double-crossed," Bond said to The Bull. The big man replied by grinning broadly, revealing his shiny, gold teeth.

"Zukovsky? He was a terrible boss. Long hours and no benefits," he said. "I got a new job now. More responsibility and better pay. Get in."

Bond and Christmas got into the car, packed between both bodyguards, and were taken away.

14

One Last Screw

An innocent-looking launch coasted to the Maiden's Tower and docked. A tarpaulin was raised so that Bond and Christmas, their hands bound, could be led by The Bull and Gabor into their prison.

"Move," The Bull commanded, his gun digging into Bond's back.

Bond looked around furtively before being ushered inside, but there were no other vessels about that might have seen them.

Take it one step at a time, he thought.

They entered the ancient monument and stood in the magnificent entry hall. The light from the stained-glass windows created a somber ambience that amplified

Bond's feeling of dread. The showdown would certainly take place here.

The sound of footsteps on the stone stairs alerted them to her presence. Elektra fluttered down and met them, much too jubilantly.

"Welcome to Istanbul, James," she said. "Did you have a comfortable journey? I hope you haven't been mistreated. Yet." She looked at Christmas. "I see you've made a new friend. How lovely. We'll make sure she gets the same first-class treatment that you do."

"You're all heart," Bond said.

She smiled coldly at the two captives. "Take them upstairs," she told Gabor. "Don't worry, James, I'll come and give you a proper hello in a moment. There's something I must attend to first."

Bond simply glared at her as the men shoved them forward.

In another room in the monument, Renard checked his watch and nodded to his men.

"That should be enough time," he said. "Let's go."

They went down the passage to the hidden quay, hopped onto the platform and boarded the bridge of the submarine. They climbed through the open hatch and descended into the eerie, dark boat. It was like being in a sepulchre: the lighting was green and sickly and the silence was unnerving.

Renard made his way to the mess, where he found Captain Nikolai and several men hunched over the table or lying on the floor. Half-eaten sandwiches and empty glasses of brandy lay scattered around them. One man had vomited and was lying in the stench. They all wore wide-eyed, frozen masks of terror.

"The poison worked fast," one of Renard's men said.

"Take them up and throw them in the sea," Renard commanded. "Search the entire sub, we don't want to miss anyone."

As they dragged Nikolai away, his captain's hat fell to the floor. Renard picked it up and put it on his head. A perfect fit.

"We'll be under way in two hours. Use that time to ponder how rich you'll be," he told his men.

One of them handed Renard the heavy lead case.

"The plutonium, sir," he said, straining with the effort.

Renard took the box as if it was nothing. He had become stronger than ever. He handed it to Truhkin, who did his best not to show how heavy it was.

"You'll find the extruder in the chamber outside the reactor," Renard said. "Better get to work."

Truhkin grunted and moved through the hatch.

After they had scoured the ship, Renard disembarked and found Elektra waiting at the quay. He ordered his men to go up into the tower and get their things and be back in ten minutes.

"The reactor is secured," he told Elektra. "Everything is ready. As planned. Is your helicopter ready?"

"It's coming to pick me up in a half hour," she replied.

He glanced around the chamber and saw that they were alone. He stepped closer to her and looked into her eyes. It was the moment he had dreaded for weeks. He reached out and lovingly caressed her hair.

"This is the end," he said softly.

"No. It is the beginning. The world will never be the same."

"I wish I could see it with you."

She hesitated, but then said, "So . . . so do I."

He could feel her reluctance to show him any affection. As much as he wanted to take her into his arms and kiss her, he resisted the urge. If she wanted to play it cool, then so be it.

Renard removed the captain's hat. Despite the frozen half of his expressionless face, it was impossible to hide his sorrow. He attempted to touch her cheek but stopped himself—catching his hand in midair—and decided, instead, to wave her off.

"The future is yours. Have fun with it."

Renard handed her the hat, turned away, and walked back to the sub.

Elektra watched him go with mixed emotions. She wanted to lash out at him, but at the same time she wanted to cradle the man in her arms. As he went through the hatch, he stopped and gave her one more longing look. She could have sworn there were tears in his eyes. She felt a lump in the middle of her chest, and for a terrible few seconds, she struggled against running to him.

Renard mouthed the word "good-bye," then disappeared into the sub. Elektra almost involuntarily cried out; she felt as if a part of her spirit was clawing its way out of her body. *Damn it all!* she thought. She was above this! Now was not the time for weakness! She had no use for "feelings" now!

Elektra coldly cast away whatever warmth still remained in her soul. From that moment on, her heart became a block of ice. It was a confusing and unpleasant sensation, and it made her angry. She had to divert the rage before it consumed her, and she knew just where she could redirect it.

Following Elektra's instructions, Gabor took Bond and Christmas to her bedroom and forced Bond to sit in an ornately carved, wooden straight-back chair. His hands were bound in cuffs attached to the sides of the seat. He struggled with them, but the cuffs kept him constrained. Christmas was standing nearby with her hands tied in front of her, a guard watching her every move.

"What happens now?" Bond asked. "The old 'Gloating-Followed-by-Torture-Followed-by-More-Gloating' routine?"

Right on cue, Elektra entered the room, threw down the captain's hat, crossed the floor, and kissed Bond on the cheek as she eyed Christmas.

"James Bond!" she said, ever so sweetly. "If only you'd kept away, we might have met again in a few years and become lovers once more."

Christmas furrowed her brow at this. Elektra turned to her. "That's right, dear. I said 'lovers.' Don't tell me that you thought you were going to get James all to yourself? Haven't you heard? James Bond is the world's biggest pig. He's a sexy pig, I'll grant you that, but he's still a pig." She nodded to Gabor. "Take her to Renard and leave us alone. I'm sure he'll find a way to amuse her for the last hour of her life. Say bon voyage, my dear."

There was fear in Christmas's eyes as the men took her away. After the door slammed shut, Bond could see their shadows move past the colorful stained-glass window and heard their footsteps echo in the stairwell.

Elektra moved to a large curved window that overlooked the whole of Istanbul.

"Pretty thing," she said. "You had her, too?"

Bond ignored the question.

"You should never have rejected me, James. I could have given you the world," she said spitefully.

"The world is not enough," he said wearily.

"Foolish sentiment."

"Family motto," he explained.

She frowned and slinked toward him. Slowly, she leaned over him and ran her fingers through his hair. Her scent was strong and musky.

"Isn't this a lovely monument? It took some doing for my father to rent it. The Turkish government didn't want to let him have it. When he convinced them that their oil was more important than their history, they gave in."

She moved in closer and nibbled his ear.

"Mmm, you *are* delicious, James. It's really too bad we've taken opposite sides in all this."

"It's not too late to change your mind," he suggested.

"Don't kid yourself, James. You're doomed and you know it."

She ran her fingernails down his right cheek, tracing the outline of the faint scar.

"They were digging near here and they found some

very pretty vases. They also found this chair . . ." She casually reached behind his neck and unwound a leather strap from the back of the chair. It was attached to the chair with a wooden screw. "I think we ignore the old ways at our peril, don't you?"

She fastened the garrote tight around Bond's neck, looked at him lovingly, and then turned the screw a notch. The effect on Bond was instantaneous as the bolt jolted into the back of his neck, tilting his head back. The idea was not only to strangle him, but to pierce his spinal cord as well.

He stared back at her. "Where's M?"

"Soon she'll be everywhere."

Bond kept his cool. "All this, because you fell for Renard?" he asked.

"Seven more turns and your neck will break." She moved to the back of the chair and twisted the screw one notch. Now the pain was more noticeable.

"I didn't fall for Renard. He fell for *me*. Since I was a child, I've always had a power over men. When I realized my father wouldn't rescue me from the kidnappers, I knew I had to form a new alliance."

He realized what she really meant. "You turned Renard."

"Just like you," she said, smiling. "Only you were even easier."

She removed the jewel from her ear and revealed the ugly scar that divided her earlobe.

"I told him he had to hurt me, he had to make it look real. When he refused, I told him I would do it myself. So I did."

She reached behind him and turned the screw another notch.

Sweat was beginning to bead on Bond's forehead. His eyes narrowed and he spat, "So it's true. *You* killed your father."

"He killed me! First he killed my mother with his neglect! He took her family's oil fields, and then he abandoned her. She died a lonely, unhappy woman. Then he killed *me* the day he refused to pay my ransom!" It was an outburst of emotions that she had thus far been able to conceal. Bond was getting to her.

He understood now. Renard had kidnapped her, hoping to get a five-million-dollar ransom out of it. When Sir Robert didn't pay up, she felt betrayed and decided to strike back. She had used her seductive charms on Renard and convinced him to enter an evil pact with her to destroy her father and take over the company.

"I was already in the process of planning how to get rid of my father when I got kidnapped," she admitted. "At first, I was frightened—being bound, gagged, and blindfolded, and taken against my will—but it ended up being a stroke of luck for me. I was able to, as you say, turn poor Renard. I quickly saw the potential in securing his devotion. I could let him do all the dirty work. He was a vicious killer, yet I was able to find his weakness and exploit it. Like anyone, all Renard needed was a little affection. A man will do just about anything for love, wouldn't you agree?"

"Was this all about the oil?"

"It is *my* oil! Mine and my mother's! It runs in my veins, thicker than blood." Her eyes were shining. She moved toward the view, gazing at the spectacular cradle of civilization. All the while, Bond worked at the wristbands feverishly.

"It was already yours, Elektra. Why are you doing all this?"

"I'm going to redraw the map. And when I am through, the whole world will know my name, my mother's name, the glory of my people."

"No one will believe this meltdown was an accident."

She turned back toward him, impressed that he had worked out the plan. She lashed her hand out and tightened the screw another notch. Now he was having trouble breathing. The point was digging into the back of his neckbone.

"They will believe," she said with amazing confidence. "They will all believe."

Another notch. Agony! Sweat was pouring off his face now as he struggled to keep focused.

"You understand? Nobody can resist me." She put the jewel back on her ear, then straddled his lap. "Not even you. Know what happens when a man is strangled?" she purred.

"Elektra . . ." Bond strained to speak. "It's not too late. Eight million people needn't die."

She smiled and twisted the screw again. There was a nasty, grinding sound as Bond winced. He closed his eyes, then forced himself to remain as cool as possible. He felt her tongue gently lick the sweat away from his brow.

"You should have killed me when you had the

chance," she whispered. "But you couldn't. Not me. A woman you've loved."

She pushed her pelvis into his. She could feel him beneath her as she rocked back and forth, breathing heavily.

"Two more . . . turns . . . and it's over, James," she said.

She twisted the screw, this time causing him extreme agony. His face was angled upward but he managed to spit, "You meant . . . nothing . . . to me . . ."

She fingered the bolt and prepared to turn the last time. His hands strained at the bindings . . .

"One . . . last . . . screw . . . ?" he choked.

She kissed his ear as she reached a climax. "Oh, James . . ." she moaned almost sadly as she began to turn the screw.

Bond was on the edge of consciousness . . . but the sound of gunfire outside brought him back to reality.

Elektra froze. She caught her breath and listened. Then she stood up abruptly and moved to the window.

Outside, Valentin Zukovsky was getting off a boat and moving over rocks toward the entrance with three of his men. He was big, battered, and bloody. All four of them were firing automatic weapons, killing anything in sight. Two of Elektra's guards lay dead in his trail. The man was obviously determined to get inside and nothing was going to stop him.

The sound of gunfire was now inside the building and moving up the stairs. Elektra reached into a desk and retrieved a Browning 9mm just as the stained-glass window shattered. Gabor, his body full of holes, fell through to the floor and caused a puddle of blood to spread over the stone. Two of Elektra's men stepped backward into the room, firing at their opponents on the stairs. Zukovsky's firepower was too much, though, and the two men were flung backward in a hail of bullets.

Then Zukovsky crashed through the broken glass, wounded in the shoulder, his face set. He had a gun in one hand and his cane in the other. He saw Bond in the chair and looked at Elektra, who was holding the gun behind her back.

There was more gunfire outside the room. Zukovsky turned to see The Bull, who entered the room holding an AK-47.

"Boss!" The Bull said. "I'm glad to see you alive! These people tricked me into—"

Zukovsky shot him without batting an eyelid. The Bull grunted and let off a round of fire, but his aim was way off the mark. He fell to the floor with a solid thud.

Zukovsky turned back to Elektra. "I'm looking for a submarine. It's big and black, and the driver is a friend of mine."

Then his eye fell on the captain's hat on the floor. Knowing at once what this meant, he ordered, "Bring it to me." He pointed the gun at her.

Elektra nodded and picked up the hat, surreptitiously sliding the Browning beneath it.

She proffered the hat and said, "What a shame. You just missed him."

Elektra let off three rounds through the hat. They slammed into Zukovsky's chest, throwing him back to the wall. He stared with incomprehension, then slumped to the floor.

Elektra walked to him and pushed his gun away from him with her toe.

Seconds away from death, Zukovsky dredged up every last ounce of energy to raise his cane a millimeter off the ground. He rested the handle against his chest and pointed the tip directly at Bond. Elektra watched curiously as Zukovsky grasped the center of the stick and stared at the man in the torture chair.

Bond gazed back. Zukovsky's eye narrowed, then he pulled back on the stick as if it were a pump-action shotgun. A single shot splintered the wood on the back of Bond's chair. What Elektra didn't notice was that the bullet had cleanly cut through the clasp binding one of Bond's wrists. A brilliant shot!

A silent acknowledgment passed between the two men. Comrades-in-arms. The merest of smiles. Then the light faded from Zukovsky's eyes and his head rolled forward.

Elektra stared at the Russian with confusion. She didn't see where the bullet had gone, only that it had missed Bond.

She sighed and turned back to Bond. "Excuse me a moment." She picked up a walkie-talkie and spoke into it. "Everything's under control up here. Are you ready?"

"Yes," came Renard's voice. "I was afraid that you—"

"I'm all right. You had better get on with it."

"Very well. *Au revoir . . .*"

"Good-bye," she said. Lost for a moment, she

breathed heavily. She dropped the walkie-talkie, glanced at Zukovsky's corpse, then back at Bond.

"Zukovsky really hated you, didn't he?" she said, slightly puzzled. She then moved back to the chair and straddled his lap again. "Time to say your prayers."

She kissed him, long and hard, then reached behind to deliver the killing twist . . .

In a lightning-fast move, Bond's hand broke free and grabbed her throat tightly. He held her, their faces close together, disdain in his eyes. He then hurled her backward, her nails scratching his face as she went.

She was momentarily stunned. Bond quickly reached over and freed his other hand, then tugged at the garrote, loosening it until he was able to slip it off. He got to his feet, but by then Elektra had recovered, run out of the room, and was ascending the stairs. He went to Zukovsky, felt his pulse, then picked up the bloody gun.

He took the walkie-talkie and had a moment's hesitation—should he race below to the submarine, or follow Elektra?

He decided to go after the girl. The bitch had gone too far . . .

Outside, at the quay, the submarine's engines roared into life.

15

Unholy Alliance

As he felt the powerful engines rumble throughout the submarine, Victor Zokas, a.k.a. Renard the Fox, felt the bullet in his skull vibrate. Of course, he knew it was not really an actual "feeling," for his nerves were completely dead there. It was what that Syrian doctor had warned him about—the kind of sensation one felt at a dentist's office after being given Novocain. The dentist would always say, "What you'll feel is a bit of pressure . . ." That was precisely what Renard felt. Pressure.

He had noticed some physical changes over the last twenty-four hours that he hadn't mentioned to Elektra. While his strength and tolerance to pain were increasing by the minute, his capacity to smell, taste, and touch was all but extinguished. The foolish doctor had told him that his sensory abilities would almost certainly degenerate rapidly just before "the end." Renard hadn't liked what he'd been told by the idiotic doctor who couldn't remove the bullet, so he had strangled him.

Renard looked around the sub's control room and noted that *his* skeleton crew were at their positions. Two men here. One in the tank room. A man in the torpedo room. They believed they were going to get rich and return home. Little did they know that they were on a collision course with destiny. The sub was moving and there was no stopping it. All was going according to plan. Everything was fine.

So why did he feel so lousy? Was that what was happening to him? Was he dying? Had the end come already?

He tested his reflexes by performing some simple exercises with his fingers and hands. They seemed to be working fine. He could see perfectly well. His hearing had not been affected. He just felt . . . out of body, somehow. It was as if he had separated from his physical self and was looking down upon the world. Nothing seemed real.

Well, he thought, if this was the end, then he was going to see the mission completed before it happened. If that meant speeding up the schedule, so be it.

He couldn't help wondering about what was going on in the tower. Elektra had sounded breathless on the radio, even though she said everything was under control. Had Bond escaped? Surely not. Elektra had been looking forward to making the MI6 agent die slowly and painfully. Perhaps she was simply feeling the excitement of nearing her goal.

Renard thought back over the past year and how he had changed as a human being. Before meeting Elektra King, he had been a bitter, loveless man who had cared about nothing but anarchy. He had never been successful with women. A prison psychiatrist once told him that his penchant for evil was due to some sort of lack of affection he had experienced when he was a child.

Renard thought about his mother, a bar tart in Moscow. She had never been at home to look after him and his three older sisters. Each of the siblings could have claimed a different father. Renard never knew his own.

His mother often came home late at night, drunk and irritable. He could vividly recall the smell of alcohol and smoke that wafted into the small, dank flat where they all lived. There was always something that she found to shout about: one of his sisters had forgotten to do the laundry, another sister hadn't cleaned the toilet, he hadn't scrubbed the floors.

Sometimes his sisters would blame him for the minor transgressions. His mother would beat him, and his siblings would watch and laugh. God, how he hated them all.

He was no psychiatrist, but even Renard could understand why he might have a problem with women.

Another memory suddenly flooded into his brain. He was fourteen, and he had decided to leave his family and fend for himself on the streets. He had crept into his mother's bedroom, thinking she was asleep in a drunken stupor. She awoke and caught him stealing money from her handbag. She chased after him, but he ran outside, without a coat or any belongings, and never came back. It was the last time he had seen his mother.

He saw his eldest sister once, two years later. She had been looking for him all over Moscow. It was pure chance that they ran into each other at a shelter that was handing out food for the needy. She told him that a drunken sailor in a tavern had murdered their mother. The three girls had split up and each was on her own. Two of them were working as prostitutes. She had managed to get a job as a seamstress. They were penniless. His sister begged him to come to their aid.

Renard, who hadn't forgotten the cruelty his sisters had shown him, refused to help. He walked away from his family and never looked back.

When he was eighteen, the Soviet army caught up with him. Surprisingly, he took to the vigorous routine and applied himself in all aspects of military life. He became adept with firearms, learned how to make explosives, and mastered hand-to-hand combat. He enjoyed training exercises and was reprimanded twice for taking "simulations" dangerously close to reality. One time, he killed two fellow recruits and made it look like an accident. It had been a pleasurable experience knowing that he could control life and death in that way. In many ways, he was a problem for the Soviet army. He had aggressive tendencies that were often disturbing and disruptive. He was mean-spirited and made no friends. But once the officials realized that they had a cold-blooded killer on their hands, they moved Renard from the regular army into a special branch of army intelligence.

The position was much more to Renard's liking and temperament. He worked as an assassin and explosives expert until the collapse of the Soviet Union. Among his many accomplishments was the murder of at least three MI6 agents, four CIA men, and seven from the Mossad. He had kept a chart on the wall of his room in the barracks in Moscow, marking off "kills" as he made them.

After the USSR broke up, he went AWOL, left Russia, and found that his reputation had preceded him nearly everywhere he went. Obtaining freelance mercenary jobs was incredibly easy. He especially enjoyed working for anticapitalist groups who wanted to see the return of communism. At least it was something to believe in. He became more publicly outspoken, issuing grand statements and warnings when he committed an atrocity.

Renard had gained the unwanted nickname "the Fox" after a particularly successful espionage operation that he had carried out in Iran. He was recognized as having a knack for stealth and secrecy. He had the ability to infiltrate the most impenetrable places, perform all manners of covert activities or violence, and leave without a trace. It wasn't long before he was on the American FBI's most wanted list of worldwide terrorists and anarchists. He was arrested only once, in Korea, and was extradited to Russia. That was where he had met the psychiatrist who had told him he had a problem with women.

Renard's first sexual experience hadn't occurred until

he was eighteen years old, which was late by most standards. It was not a pleasant experience. The prostitute taunted him, made fun of his thinning hair, and enjoyed humiliating him when he was unable to perform. .

The second experience was a rape. It was a crime that, fortunately for him, went unsolved. It was in Warsaw, and Renard had followed a young girl home from a bakery, forced her into an alley, and viciously had his way with her.

It had left him completely unsatisfied.

The third experience convinced him that he just couldn't "hit it off" with women, and he had to accept it. She was a fellow mercenary, ten years older than he, a tough, idealistic communist who had an ugly, shrapnel scar across her face. Otherwise not unattractive, the woman seemed to take a shine to him. She managed to seduce him, but the lovemaking was awkward and self-conscious. It ended with a quarrel, and he killed her.

From then on, Renard tried to ignore women as sexual beings, but he found that he desired them more than ever. He would stare at photos of supermodels and become attached to glamorous movie stars. He fantasized about someday having a beautiful woman in his control.

When he discovered that Sir Robert King, the wealthy oil tycoon, had a daughter . . . he knew he could fulfill that fantasy.

He first saw her in a British financial magazine. It was an article about King Industries and how Elektra was following in her father's footsteps. In the photo, she was wearing a business suit, but with a short skirt, and was standing in the middle of a group of workmen. She exuded confidence and authority. He fell in love with her at first sight.

Further investigation into Sir Robert King revealed that he might be a worthwhile target for ransom. Renard hired four stooges to help him, and they moved into an abandoned cottage in Dorset to carry out their plan to extort five million dollars from the tycoon.

But Renard had an ulterior motive. He wanted to meet Elektra King and see her in the flesh. He wanted to touch her skin, smell her hair . . . taste her mouth.

He watched her as she came and went from the King Industries office in London. She was then living in a small flat in the Mayfair area and it didn't take long to memorize her daily routine, which rarely changed. Renard and his men abducted her in broad daylight one morning as she left her flat.

They drove to Dorset with her kicking and struggling in the back of a van. He had to hit her a few times, but she finally settled down. By the time they had locked her in the cold, damp room in the cottage, she was frightened and vulnerable.

And oh, so beautiful . . .

He attempted to talk to her during the first couple of days. She refused to speak. Once she spat at him. He slapped her and left the room.

The first ransom demand went out on the second day of her captivity. Sir Robert's response was that he needed "more time." When Elektra heard that, she was shocked.

"More time?" she asked. "For what? He *has* the money!"

From then on, her attitude had changed. When food was brought to her, she would request that Renard himself bring it. Sometimes she asked that he sit and talk with her while she ate. She no longer seemed afraid of him.

Renard enjoyed watching her and listening to her, so he didn't mind. He knew that he was falling for his captive, but he was careful not to let it show. He now understood that Elektra could see right through him and knew which buttons to push.

She was the most intelligent woman he had ever met.

After seven days of captivity, word was received that Sir Robert "still needed more time" to pay the ransom. It was obvious that he was stalling. A source on the street had told Renard that Sir Robert had contacted MI6 for help in the matter. When Elektra heard this, she became furious.

"Am I not worth a measly five million dollars? That amount of money is nothing to him!"

That night, something extraordinary happened, and he would never forget it as long as he lived.

Elektra asked for him and specifically requested that he bring a bucket of ice and a bottle of champagne. When he entered her room, she was beneath the sheets of the bed and was wearing absolutely nothing.

Slowly and sensuously, Elektra King seduced Renard. At first he was apprehensive and nervous, terribly afraid that he would have yet another bad experience. Elektra alleviated his fears. She was no innocent. She was extremely skilled in the pleasures of the flesh.

The one thing she did that got him to relax was using

the ice. She had made him watch her as she took a frozen sliver and rubbed it all over her body, letting the water dribble over her smooth, soft skin. She used it to arouse herself, make her nipples hard, and stimulate her senses. Renard was hypnotized by her act, and he found himself so tantalized that for the first time in his life he was able to have normal sexual relations with a woman.

From then on, he was the slave and she was the master. He made no bones about it. He pledged his devotion and servitude to her, and promised to do anything her heart desired.

That was when she made him a business proposition.

"How would you like to kill my father?" she had asked.

She explained that she wanted King Industries for herself so that she could reclaim her mother's oil. She had grand ideas to create a worldwide oil monopoly.

Renard had thought about it for a couple of days. In the interim, Elektra would skillfully outline her plans for him, how he would fit into her life, and how they would be lovers.

She discussed with him the possibility of a "new world order" in which they were the masters. To accomplish that, Istanbul and the Bosphorus would have to be destroyed. This would close off the existing oil pipelines to the West, leaving the King Industries source as the only one. She would be the most powerful woman on earth.

Elektra offered Renard the chance to be her right-hand man if he helped her devise a way to carry out her plan.

The first step was to stage her escape. After three

weeks of captivity, Elektra thought the most believable scenario would be that she had gotten lucky and overcome the guards. She was not afraid to say that she used her body to seduce a guard, kick him in the groin, and then take his gun. Renard would conveniently be away at the time, thereby allowing him to live to see another day. In fact, it was Renard who killed his own men— he was that much under her spell. He would have done anything she asked.

They had been fairly useless henchmen anyway.

Elektra had shown great courage when it came time to make it look as if she had been beaten. She forced him to hit her three times in the face, bloodying her nose and giving her a black eye.

"There have to be signs of torture, Renard," she had told him. "Otherwise no one will believe me. It would have been too easy."

She held out a pair of wire cutters and ordered him to cut her ear. Renard refused to hurt her again.

"Come on, you do this kind of thing to other people all the time," she taunted, but still he shunned the notion.

"I cannot harm one hair on your head," he told her. The woman enraptured him, and he didn't mind admitting it. There were times when he wanted to run out into the streets of London and shout out that he was in love. He wanted to show his old schoolmates that he, too, could have a lover. If only his stupid mother and sisters could see him now . . .

"If you won't do it, then I'll have to," she said.

"It will hurt you," he said.

"There's no point in living if you can't feel alive," she replied.

Without so much as a flinch, Elektra stood in front of a mirror, held the cutters to her earlobe, then snapped once. The blood spurted everywhere. She didn't cry out in pain. Renard couldn't remember for certain, but she may have even laughed when she saw all the blood.

They bandaged her up, made certain that she looked the part of an abused kidnap victim, and said good-bye. He left for Russia—she walked out of the cottage, leaving three dead bodies, and flagged down a lorry on the main road nearby.

The second step was to get rid of her father. Renard, with his connections in Russia, was able to set up the phony sale of the Russian Atomic Energy report to Sir Robert and arrange for a "refund." He had rigged the money with explosives. They had agreed to wait a year before committing the crime. It was safer that way. Unfortunately, in the meantime, the MI6 agent in Syria had wounded Renard in the head. Nevertheless, the murder of Sir Robert went off without a hitch.

The next step was to obtain a weapon so that they could steal some plutonium. Renard was able to hijack a Russian army transport plane and steal an atomic bomb from under the noses of the military and the IDA. His reputation as "the Fox" had come in handy in that regard. Elektra used her own influence to get hold of a Russian submarine. Everything had worked beautifully.

If only the damned MI6 agent hadn't shot him in the head. If only he was still able to feel. If only he wasn't on a one-way road to hell. Otherwise, he might be able to sit with Elektra on her throne of power once all of this was over. He might have been able to keep her love. He wouldn't have had to let the bastard Bond have his way with her. Nevertheless, Renard looked at that episode as a token of his compassion for her. An offering. Since he was unable to give Elektra pleasure anymore, why should he deny her needs? She was a very physical person. He knew that she was attracted to the British agent. That night after the casino . . . he could have killed Bond then and there. But his love for Elektra prevented him from doing so. He wanted to give her a night of pleasure, even if it was with the enemy.

Now he sat in the sub, ready to dive and finish what they had begun over a year earlier, and all he felt was an overwhelming sadness. They had said their goodbyes, Elektra and he. He would never see her again. He would go down with the sub, hopefully preventing a possible painful death from the ever-present bullet in his brain. It was the ultimate sacrifice. He was doing it for love.

It was possibly the noblest thing he had ever done in his life.

Someday, after she had lived a long and fruitful life . . . they would renew their loving alliance in hell.

16

Countdown to Oblivion

Bond chased Elektra up the triple spiral staircase leading to the minaret's balconies.

"James. You can't kill me. Not in cold blood," her voice echoed in the stone chamber.

Bond wasn't wavering. He clutched Zukovsky's bloody, wet gun and ascended in the semidarkness. As he swung around a corner of a landing, he heard an unexpected but familiar voice.

"Bond!"

He stopped and kicked at the door. The room was empty except for the barred cell at one end. M, looking tired, breathed a sigh of relief.

Bond shot at the lock on the cell door, blowing it to bits.

"Are you all right?" he asked her.

"Yes," she said, leaving her prison. "I just—"

But Bond had already turned to go, heading upward, after Elektra.

"Go after the submarine!" M called after him. "Forget the girl! Bond!"

Elektra reached the uppermost balcony, which afforded a spectacular view of the Bosphorus and the city beyond. She stood there, looking out at the sea as the submarine pulled out of the quay. Bond stepped behind her; she had no way of escape.

"Call him off," he said, holding the walkie-talkie to her.

Elektra turned around to face him.

"I won't ask again. Call him off!"

She looked at him questioningly. Did he really mean it? Hesitantly, she took the radio and held it to her mouth.

This is your last chance, Bond thought. *Save the city. Save yourself.*

"Renard . . ." she said into the radio.

Bond waited.

"You wouldn't kill me," she whispered to Bond. "You'd miss me."

Then her face broke into a perverted grin and she shouted into the radio, "Dive! Dive! Bond is—"

The force of the bullet knocked her back against the balcony rail. She dropped the radio and stared at Bond in disbelief. He had actually shot her.

"I never miss," Bond said.

Elektra King slumped to the floor, shocked by her

own mortality. Gasping for breath, she looked up at Bond. She was attempting to say something. Bond crouched beside her and listened, but he couldn't understand the words. She was speaking—no, she was singing!—singing in a whisper. It sounded like a lullaby.

After half a minute, she choked once and shuddered. There might have been a hint of regret in her watering eyes, but this quickly vanished as a cold, dark shadow passed over her face. Whatever demons had been tormenting her were now gone. She attempted to complete the verse of the lullaby, but could only manage a final exhalation of breath.

Bond looked at the lovely face, now relaxed and in peace; he reached out and caressed her cheek, just once.

Behind him, in the doorway, M had seen it all. She hardened her heart to the swirling cacophony of emotions that yearned to cry out for the poor, tortured girl. Bond had done his duty, but M couldn't help saying a silent prayer for the soul of Elektra King.

Bond stood, looked over the rail to see the nose of the submarine heading into the Bosphorus, half-submerged. The hatch was still open. He stepped onto the ledge and prepared himself. Without a second thought, he performed a flawless swan dive, one hundred feet to the water. He hit it like a knife and found it very cold. He surfaced near the sub, grabbed a ladder, and pulled himself up. Splashing through the water that was flooding over the rail, he appeared in front of the amazed sailor who was just shutting the hatch. Bond slammed the lid on the man's head, then crawled inside. He closed it and turned the wheel seconds before the hatch slid underwater.

Bond crept down into the dark vessel. Renard's small crew was spread throughout the sub, so he knew the best tactic was silence. He peered into the control room and saw Renard and several men at various stations. Beyond them, on the other side, were the outer chambers of the machine room and reactor room.

He moved toward the bow and down a ladder to what appeared to be living quarters. He found one man working on a radio and smoking a cigarette. Bond's gun barrel dug into the man's temple.

"Easy," he said. "How do you want to die? That?" He indicated the cigarette. "Or this?" He pressed the barrel harder into the man's head. "One word and your brains will be on the floor. Now—take me to the girl they brought on board."

The man's cigarette dropped from his mouth as he nodded in compliance. He led Bond forward and down another ladder to a crew room. He pointed to a solid metal door.

"She's in there?" Bond asked.

The man nodded.

"You have the key?"

The man offered it.

"Thanks. Now we'll knock, all right?"

The man nodded again.

Bond took hold of the man's head and banged it hard on the door, rendering him unconscious. He then unlocked the door and found Christmas Jones sitting on a cot.

"James!" she said, stunned to see him.

He untied her bonds, put his finger to his lips, and then led her through the shadows of the sub toward the control room. They soon came upon the tank room and found a man operating them.

Renard's voice came over the intercom. "Flood tanks four and five . . ."

"Flooding tanks four and five," the man said into a radio on the table, then he did as he was told. As soon as he was finished, Bond knocked him out with the butt of his gun.

"We have to get to the reactor room," he said. "It's on the other side of the control room, but Renard and his men are in there."

"Is there another way?" Christmas asked.

"We go down to the torpedo bay."

Before they could move, though, a man entered through a hatch. Bond lashed out at him, but the man's reflexes were sharp. He deflected Bond's blow and rebounded with a vicious kick to Bond's chest. Bond dropped his gun and it slid across the floor.

Christmas watched helplessly as the two men fought silently and ferociously. The man drew his gun but Bond kicked it out of his hand. This was followed by a solid punch to the man's face, sending him sprawling over the table where the radio sat. He reached for the fire alarm, but Bond grabbed his legs and pulled him off the table. The man used the momentum to twist and elbow Bond in the stomach.

"Open the tanks," Renard's voice said over the intercom.

Hunched over, Bond propelled himself forward and knocked the man back onto the table. He grabbed the radio receiver and wrapped the coiled cable around the man's neck, throttling him.

"Open the tanks. Do you copy?" Renard's voice came again.

Bond pulled the cable tighter. The man's eyes bulged. Disguising his voice, Bond pushed the transmit button on the microphone and said, "Tanks open."

The man finally slumped to the floor. Christmas was obviously shaken. Bond retrieved his gun, took her hand, and led her forward.

Unaware of the situation in another part of the boat, Renard left the control room momentarily and joined Truhkin in the machine room. Truhkin was hard at work with the extruder, a machine that resembled a gigantic V-8 engine. He carefully lifted the half-grapefruit-sized plutonium core from the metal box, then placed it inside the extruder, which would mold the substance into the shape of a reactor control rod. Satisfied that the procedure was going smoothly, Renard left Truhkin to his business and returned to the control room.

Bond and Christmas found a hatch with a small window looking into the control room. Bond peered in and saw five crewmen at different consoles. Renard was pacing among them.

"Level out at one hundred feet," he commanded. "Hold her steady."

The crewman closest to Bond operated the buoyancy controls. The helmsman, across the room, reduced the engine thrust. Renard felt the submarine's position change, nodded, and went back through the hatch toward the reactor room.

Bond whispered to Christmas, "If we could force them to the surface, it would show up on the spy satellites. That would bring out the navy. Wait here."

"Where are you going?" she asked, wide-eyed.

"In there."

Renard rejoined Truhkin in the machine room in time to see the plutonium rod emerge from the end of the extruder.

Bond opened the hatch, stepped into the control room, and slammed the butt of his Walther into the buoyancy control crewman's head. The rest of the crew reacted, going for their guns, but Bond was faster.

"Don't even think of it," he said, covering them.

He scanned the controls at his side and saw four emergency handles that would blow the buoyancy tanks. Bond grabbed the two for the forward tanks and pulled them down.

Alarms sounded throughout the ship and a loud hiss of air could be heard everywhere. The main forward ballast tanks immediately began filling with water. Bond purposefully avoided opening the aft ballast tanks so that the submarine would dive nose first, which it did— abruptly.

Renard cursed and ran back to the control room with his gun drawn to find his crew standing frozen at their positions.

Upon seeing Bond, Renard screamed, "Shoot him!"

Everyone dived for cover as he and Bond exchanged fire, but the sub's tilting threw them off balance. The bullets ricocheted off the control panels, blowing them to pieces. Renard wedged himself in the doorway leading to the reactor room, but the other crewmen lost their footing and fell to the deck. Two crewmen fired their guns at Bond, who successfully leaped out of the way in the nick of time. The bullets shattered the buoyancy control panel, forcing Bond back into the corridor with Christmas.

"Do you know what you did in there?" she asked.

"Like riding a bike," he replied.

"What kind of bikes did you ride?" she asked.

"Just wanted to put him on edge . . ."

They started to run back toward where they had come, but two new crewmen appeared at the far end of the passageway and opened fire. Bond threw Christmas to the floor and shot at them, but the Walther was out of ammunition. Thinking quickly, he jumped on top of Christmas, held on to her, and rolled with her through an open hatch to their left. Once they were inside, Bond leaped to his feet and slammed the door shut. As they took stock of their surroundings, Bond realized that they were in the bow torpedo room.

The submarine's nose continued to dive. Bond and Christmas shifted to the side of the room as everything that wasn't screwed down began to slide. They grabbed the nearest fixed objects and hung on as the room turned ninety degrees.

"Get us level!" Renard shouted to a crewman in the control room. The man pulled on the buoyancy controls, but there was no response. The machinery had been completely demolished by the gunfire.

"It's no good!" he yelled back.

The submarine tilted further until the entire vessel was hanging vertically in the water.

Renard cursed again, then climbed up, back into the machine room, and shut the door, now at his feet. As the crewmen attempted to regain their footing, the helmsman accidentally hit the engine control, sending it to "full ahead." He crashed with the rest of the men into the wall as the submarine lunged violently toward the bottom of the sea.

Bond and Christmas fell back against the racks of torpedoes. The sound of the engines was deafening. Christmas screamed. Bond held her as he looked around the room. Emergency equipment was stowed in netting against a bulkhead near them. He pulled at the straps, emptied the netting, and thrust Christmas inside.

"Quick!" he shouted, following her into the netting.

They secured themselves just as the submarine crashed into the sandy bottom of the Bosphorus.

The boat jolted with the force of an earthquake. Renard slammed hard against the wall of the machine room. The crewmen in the control room were not so lucky. Chairs and desks broke free and crushed them against the damaged equipment.

In a few moments, it was over. There was an eerie silence, save for the occasional groan of hull stress and the wail of alarms.

Renard, dazed, looked up and saw that the extruder had slid into Truhkin and killed him . . . but he was holding the finished plutonium control rod in his clenched fists. Renard got up and wrenched it free. He then made sure that the hatch to the control room was sealed.

Bond and Christmas climbed out of the netting just as a horrible creak resounded through the chamber. A rupture at the end of the racks of torpedoes spread across the wall; water gushed toward them at a frightening rate.

"Climb!" he shouted. He pulled Christmas up and they ascended toward the control room. "Keep moving!"

As they emerged into the demolished chamber, the water was already pouring through the hatch, splashing at their feet. They struggled together to shut the hatch, but by the time they were successful, the water was up to their knees.

Meanwhile Renard climbed to the reactor room, and without flinching, he opened the cover of the glaring reactor. He was bathed in a ghostly blue light.

Renard was no nuclear physicist, but he understood enough about reactors to get the job done. A reactor's only real purpose, he knew, was to generate heat to boil water into saturated steam. The only difference between it and any other type of steam-powered turbine plant was the amount of energy concentrated in the nuclear fuel in the reactor core, as well as the complete lack of any need for air.

The process of nuclear fission was really quite simple. An atom was split and released two neutrons, generating energy as heat. When the two neutrons hit two more atoms, four more neutrons were thrown, and so on, until the result was an uncontrolled, supercritical fission reaction. An atomic explosion.

Renard knew that here in the submarine, however, the amount of energy released by the splitting atoms was controlled by "control rods" that were made of a neutron-absorbing material such as cadmium or hafnium. These rods were set to absorb the right amount of neutrons to bring the reaction into controlled, critical fission. This reaction still generated a great deal of heat, boiling water into saturated steam to power the sub's turbines, but the process could continue safely for years.

Renard stared at the glowing reactor core, transfixed momentarily by the power it held. He studied it carefully, picking out what he assumed to be the uranium fuel elements that had been formed into plates to allow maximum heat transfer to the primary coolant loop. They were mounted parallel to each other in an assembly mounted on top of a support structure in the base of the reactor vessel. In between the fuel elements were the control rods, designed to drop into place in the event of a reactor problem. The coolant of the primary loop circulated around the core, feeding the heated coolant into a steam generator. This, in turn, directed the steam into a secondary cooling loop that fed a pair of high-pressure turbines in the machinery spaces. There, the steam was condensed into water and sent back into the steam generator. The turbines were responsible for turning the main propeller shaft, as well as providing electrical power to the boat and its equipment.

Renard held the plutonium control rod and prepared himself for what he had to do. The job would have to be performed slightly ahead of schedule . . .

The submarine lurched again and threw him down. He struggled to get back up to the reactor but found it to be exhausting. For some inexplicable reason, he felt real pain on the side of his head where he had been shot. It was odd to actually feel something there after so long. Was the bullet moving? Was the time the doctor had given him now up? No! He would finish Elektra's plan!

He stared into the violet-blue heat, mesmerized by its beauty. It was almost as beautiful as she . . .

He pressed a button and one of the neutron-absorbing control rods slowly rose from the reactor. He reached out and released it from its berth, then threw it across the room. Renard carefully picked up the plutonium rod and prepared to insert it into the orifice left by the rod he had removed.

He smiled, but the pain in his head overpowered him.

Back in the control room, Christmas noticed a panel light.

"Oh my God, he's opened up the reactor." Bond studied the panel as she interpreted more lights. "And he's sealed himself in."

"And us out," Bond said.

"He's already withdrawn one of the control rods. He's going to insert the plutonium. What do we do?"

Thinking fast, Bond moved to the controls near the tanks. He took four seconds to study them, then began to hit switches. He examined a control panel that was marked, in Russian, "Forward and Aft Escape Chambers." He looked around the room and saw that the forward escape hatch was located there, as well as a cabinet on the wall.

"Look in there for rebreathers," he said, pointing. She opened the cabinet and found that they had been ripped to shreds.

"Sabotaged," she said. "No one was meant to get off the sub alive."

"I never liked those things anyway," he said. He pushed a button on the panel.

The aft escape hatch opened, high up on the sub. Water flooded the escape chamber there, but an inner door stopped it from penetrating the submarine.

Christmas suddenly understood what he was planning to do and looked at him questioningly.

"You have a better idea?" Bond snapped. He opened the inner door to the forward escape chamber and said, "Count to twenty. When you get to twenty, push this button. It will open the inner door of the aft escape hatch. It can only be opened for a few seconds or we'll sink."

"But what if—"

"Count to twenty. I'll be there. Wait five more seconds, then press the purge button. That will empty the water out of the chamber."

He got inside the hatch and she sealed the door behind him, wrenching a lever that immediately flooded his chamber with water. Bond held his breath as the water poured in. It was extremely claustrophobic, but he had been in tight spots before.

A green light flashed on the control panel. Christmas punched a button and the outer forward escape hatch opened. Bond burst out into the dark water and began the long, torturous ascent up the outside of the submarine.

"One, one thousand, two, one thousand," Christmas began to chant.

It was very disorienting. There was very little illumination and Bond had difficulty getting his bearings
against the vast, black vertical whale next to him. He
might have gotten lost if he hadn't recognized the con-
ning tower jutting out sideways.

"Fourteen, one thousand, fifteen, one thousand . . ."

Bond's lungs felt as if they would explode. He had to
be almost there! Where was the bloody thing?

"Seventeen, one-thousand . . ."

There it was—the open hatch of the aft escape chamber! He swam inside then yanked the lever to close the
hatch.

Christmas was shivering in the rising water.

". . . Twenty, one-thousand." She pressed the button.

The inner hatch opened, and Bond collapsed into the
sub . . . but the chamber was full of water. Now all
Christmas had to do was press the purge button.

Before she could do so, however, the hatch leading to
the deck above split open with a tremendous shriek. She
was hit with a torrent of water, knocking her off her
feet.

In the chamber above, Bond was running out of
breath. *Where the hell is she? Press the purge button!*

Christmas struggled to get back to the controls, but
she tripped over the body of a dead seaman. She recoiled
in terror, then realized the man couldn't hurt her. The
water was rising quickly, now over her head. She ducked
into it, reached for the controls, and hit the button.

Bond rolled out into the corridor just as Christmas
closed the door. He took a few seconds to catch his
breath, then began the descent to the reactor chamber. It

took him four minutes to get there, only to find the door sealed.

Now what? he thought. Cursing to himself, he looked around the room and noticed a sign that read EMERGENCY USE ONLY. There were some lengthy instructions about when and how to open the door in case of a problem, and they were clearly marked with "Danger" warnings. Bond pulled the lever and the hatch to the reactor room exploded off its hinges.

Bond crawled into the chamber and saw that Renard was lying in a crumpled heap, unconscious. The plutonium rod was lying beside him and there was a flare gun attached to his belt. Bond took the gun and stuck it in his waistband, then moved to the controls. He saw that the temperature gauge was at four thousand degrees and climbing. A thumping noise below him got his attention. Christmas was at the window of the door. The water had risen to the top of the control room and she would drown at any moment. Bond jumped for the door and opened it.

"Christmas!" he called. He lowered an arm and pulled her up, then closed the door. Together they moved to the reactor and gazed inside.

Breathlessly, she said, "We're safe from the radiation as long as the reactor coolant doesn't burst. If he had got the plutonium in the reactor you could have written off the whole city."

Suddenly an arm locked around Bond's neck, throttling him. Behind them, Renard had regained consciousness and mustered every bit of strength to surprise-attack his enemy. Christmas grabbed at Renard, but he flung her back. She nearly fell through the hatch but managed to grab a pipe and hang on for dear life.

Bond elbowed Renard hard in the stomach. It was like hitting a stone wall. He then snapped forward, causing Renard to flip over his back. The terrorist crashed into a panel. Bond jumped on him and punched him in the face, over and over. He didn't give the man a chance to defend himself. He allowed his anger to overcome Renard's strength and really damage him—anger at what he had done to M16, anger at what he had done to Elektra . . .

After a minute of battering him, Bond snapped out of the trance. Renard was stunned. Bond pushed him away and returned to the reactor, but Renard revived quickly. The killer grabbed Bond and tossed him across the room as if he were a toy. Renard turned to ward off an ineffective blow from Christmas and back handed her over the railing. She fell against the wall, which was now the floor, and lost consciousness.

"Bond!" Renard shouted. "You have decided to join me on this historic voyage. Welcome to my nuclear family!"

Dazed, Bond shook his head and eyed the plutonium rod on the floor, just out of his reach.

"You're really going to commit suicide for her?" he asked.

"In case you've forgotten," Renard answered, "I'm dead already."

"Haven't you heard the news?" Bond spat. "So is she."

Renard's face screwed up into a grotesque mask of

pain that he would never be able to feel in his skin. His scream of bloody murder echoed throughout the ship as if a wounded animal were howling in the bowels of the boat.

Renard gasped, momentarily shaken. "You're lying."

Bond grabbed the plutonium rod, got to his feet, and swung it hard into the side of Renard's head. It barely fazed him. He took hold of Bond's shoulders and smashed him repeatedly into the steel mesh of the flooring, forcing Bond to drop the rod. Renard then threw Bond against an opening in the mesh. He fell through, dazed. Renard pulled the mesh closed and bolted it. Bond watched in frustration as the terrorist retrieved the plutonium rod.

Bond scanned the scene, searching for any idea that might save them. He saw one of the hoses that fed into the primary coolant loop had become uncoupled. It was thrashing violently nearby, as the steam passing through was under extremely high pressure. It was heated to literally hundreds of degrees and contained a great deal of motive energy.

Renard slowly inserted the plutonium rod into the reactor. Immediately the light around him became an even deeper blue, a horrible luminescence. The water coolant around the reactor core began to boil furiously.

The temperature gauge rose to 4,500 degrees.

Bond could see the end of the rod being pushed through from the other side of the reactor. There was only one thing to do. He tore a piece of fabric from his shirt and wrapped it around his hand. He then grabbed the thrashing hose and attached it to the fitting on his side of the reactor. The pressure began to build.

Renard continued to force the plutonium into the reactor as the temperature gauge neared the red-lined "5,000" mark.

Finally, the high-pressured steam dislodged the plutonium rod with such force that it shot out of the reactor and impaled Renard in the heart.

Renard stared at Bond in horror. The rod was sticking through his chest like a spear. Bond calmly said, "She's waiting for you."

Renard collapsed and fell in a heap next to Christmas, who was just beginning to regain consciousness. She recoiled at the sight of him, then gathered her wits. She got up and unbolted the steel mesh, freeing Bond, then found the original control rod lodged near the reactor. She gently picked it up and reinserted it into the fitting.

The temperature gauge immediately began to fall, but the H2 metre on the wall was in the yellow and rising toward red. Christmas spotted the needle and grabbed Bond's arm.

"The hydrogen gas level is too high. One spark and this reactor room will blow. It'll cause a disaster!"

Bond took two seconds to think, then said, "We have to flood the reactor with water. Go up to the mine room. I'll be there in a minute."

She climbed up to the next chamber as Bond opened the hatch leading to the control room. The water began to gush into the reactor chamber. Bond then fought his way to the machine-room hatch, opened it, and climbed in. He sealed the hatch behind him, preventing the water from engulfing him. He made his way forward and found Christmas in the mine room. She pointed at another H2 meter, the needle of which was in the red.

"This room is one gigantic bomb ready to explode any second. It'll set the mines off!" she cried.

"I know," Bond said. "I've sealed the reactor so it will be safe from the blast. There'll be no radiation leakage."

He motioned Christmas toward a mine launching tube.

"Get in!"

She hesitated.

"You have a better idea?" he asked.

Wide-eyed, Christmas got into the tube. Bond examined the controls, set a timer to fire, and then followed her inside. The hatch automatically closed behind them.

The clock ticked down . . .

The launching doors opened as Bond and Christmas shot out into the water, streaking away from the sub, and then upward.

Inside the now empty mine room, a torn electric cable touched the bulkhead.

The submarine blew apart with a horrendous explosion. What was left of the vessel began its slow descent to the bottom of the Bosphorus.

Bond and Christmas reached the surface, gasping for air. They looked around to see no boats coming to the rescue.

"I don't think I can tread water much longer," she cried.

"Hold on to my shoulders," he said.

A tourist boat was a hundred yards away. Bond felt in his pocket and found the flare gun that he had taken off Renard. He shot it into the air. People on the boat waved at them and turned the vessel in their direction.

17

Lullaby

Repair work on the damaged wing at SIS headquarters on the Thames was well under way. It was business as usual and had been since M had left for Castle Thane and subsequently Turkey. Bill Tanner had been left in charge, and when his chief had gone missing he had been forced to remain at the office nonstop. It hadn't been the first time that the head of SIS had been in danger, but it was the first time for *this* M. The worst thing about it was that he had been totally helpless until the locator card had pinpointed her whereabouts in Istanbul.

The M16 operatives had stormed the Maiden's Tower half an hour after the submarine had exploded. M was rescued and immediately put on an aircraft back to London. At first she had refused to go until Bond was found, but the prime minister had ordered that she return without delay.

Prior to her arrival, Tanner had a chance to sleep for a good ten hours for the first time in at least two days. Feeling fresh, he got the Briefing Room looking as if nothing untoward had occurred in her absence.

When M finally walked in, looking as efficient and steely as ever, all eyes turned to her. She looked at everyone and made the briefest of nods—all the sentiment that was allowed—and the work resumed.

Approaching Tanner, she asked, "Any word?"

"Not yet," he replied. "All we know is that Bond and Dr. Jones were picked up by a tourist boat. We have no idea where they are now."

James Bond had persuaded the captain of the tourist boat to drop them off with the other passengers so that he and Christmas could slip away surreptitiously and not have to deal with a debriefing—just yet. They took a taxi to where Q's deputy had delivered the Aston Martin, a testament to the man's foresight in providing Bond with a backup automobile. Bond drove it to a guest villa that he knew; he paid cash for two nights' rental, with the option of extending the stay. Exhausted, they had spent the rest of the day sleeping in each other's arms, then awoke to have a luxurious dinner in a nearby restaurant: *patlican kebap,* made of eggplant and lamb.

Now he held the good doctor close to him as they stood against the rail of the villa's magnificent rooftop garden that overlooked the sparkling nighttime lights of

Istanbul. It was a beautiful sight, very romantic, and James Bond had no intention of letting it go to waste.

"What's the occasion?" Christmas asked when fireworks unexpectedly exploded in the distance.

"I'm not sure," Bond said. "It's lovely, though."

"I can't remember what *month* we're in, much less what day this is."

Bond opened a bottle of Bollinger and poured two glasses.

"I always wanted to have Christmas in Turkey," he said.

She looked at him suspiciously. "Was that a Christmas joke?"

"From me? Never."

They clinked glasses and drank. The champagne was bubbly, matching their mood.

"So, isn't it time you unwrapped your present?" she asked with a wicked smile on her lips. She reclined on pillows that she had spread on the rooftop earlier.

"Have you got something?" Tanner asked the Q Branch deputy. The tall man had been sitting at a monitor for a halfhour, producing strange colors and shapes until finally the picture began to be recognizable.

"A satellite thermal image of Istanbul," he explained. "There is a minute radioactive filament in Double-0 Seven's Aston Martin. I've attempted to get a fix on that."

M stood behind them, expectantly.

The deputy zoomed in on the car, which was parked somewhere near the Golden Horn.

"He must be nearby," Tanner said.

"Where?" M asked.

The deputy maneuvered the image away from the DB5 to the villa it was parked in front of. The camera scanned the place until it focused on the garden balcony, and then on to a mass of what appeared to be cushions.

"This picks up body heat," the deputy said. "Humans should be orange." He searched the area and pointed. "There."

One orange figure was lying on the rooftop.

"I thought you said he was with Dr. Jones?" M asked Tanner.

The image began to glow darker and was moving rhythmically.

"It's getting redder," M observed. And then she realized . . . It was, of course, the image of two people, one on top of the other.

The deputy switched the screen off and cleared his throat. "Um, it could be a premature form of the Millennium Bug."

Over a thousand miles away, in the historic cradle of civilization that sat between Europe and Asia, the man and woman didn't give a second thought to who might be watching them. Instead, they were lost in each other's passion, releasing the pent-up tensions they had acquired over the last few days.

"I suppose I was wrong about you," Bond said.

She moaned softly and asked, "How so?"

"I thought Christmas came only once a year."

Their bodies melded once again into a perfect rhythm,